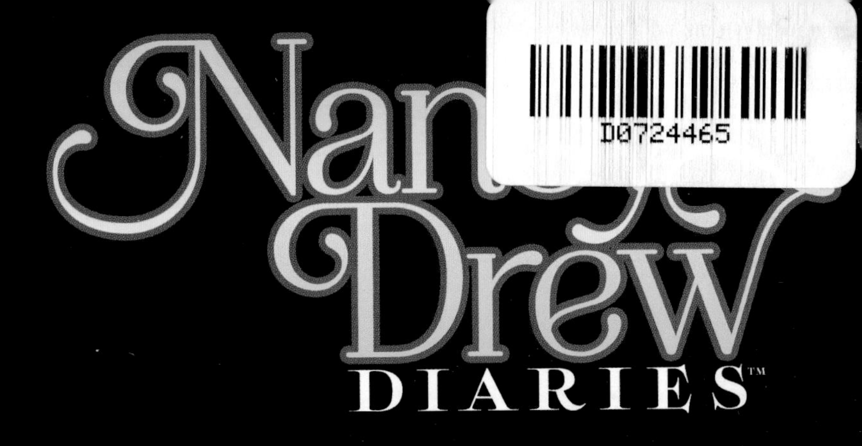

*"Bravery isn't about **not** being scared, it's about doing the right thing even if you are scared..."*

–Nancy Drew

PAPERCUTZ

NANCY DREW GRAPHIC NOVELS AVAILABLE FROM PAPERCUTZ

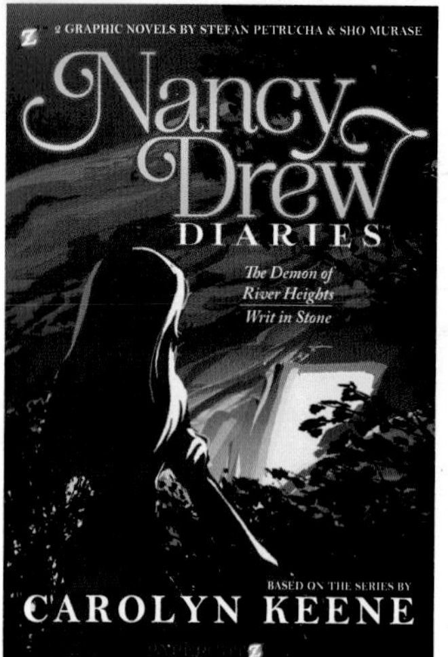

"The Demon of River Heights" and "Writ in Stone"

"The Haunted Dollhouse " and "The Girl Who Wasn't There"

#1 "The Demon of River Heights"

#2 "Writ in Stone"

#3 "The Haunted Dollhouse"

#4 "The Girl Who Wasn't There"

#5 "The Fake Heir"

#6 "Mr. Cheeters Is Missing"

#7 "The Charmed Bracelet"

#8 "Global Warning"

#9 "Ghost In The Machinery"

#10 "The Disoriented Express

#11 "Monkey Wrench Blues"

See page 175 for more NANCY DREW graphic novels!

NANCY DREW graphic novels are available at booksellers everywhere.

NANCY DREW graphic novels are $7.95 each in paperback and $12.95 each in hardcover. NANCY DREW DIARIES graphic novels are $9.99 each and available only in paperback. You may also order online at www.papercutz.com. Or call 1-800-886-1223, Monday through Friday, 9 – 5 EST. MC, Visa, and AmEx accepted. To order by mail, please add $4.00 for postage and handling for first book ordered, $1.00 for each additional book and make check payable to NBM Publishing. Send to: Papercutz, 160 Broadway, Suite 700, East Wing, New York, NY 10038.

NANCY DREW and NANCY DREW DIARIES graphic novels are also available digitally wherever e-books are sold.

papercutz.com

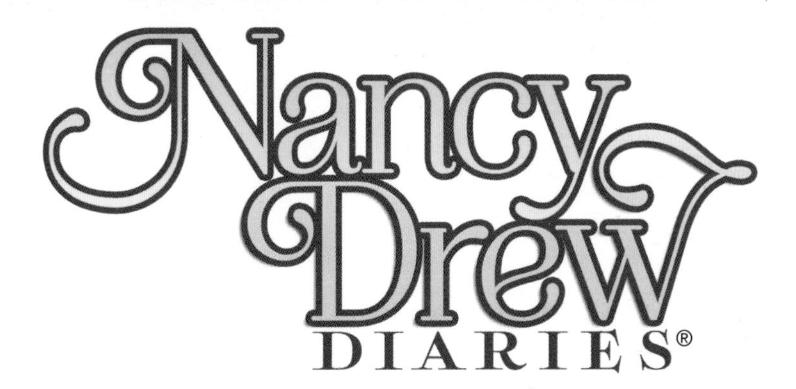

#2 "The Haunted Dollhouse"
and
"The Girl Who Wasn't There"

Based on the series by
CAROLYN KEENE
STEFAN PETRUCHA • Writer
SHO MURASE • Artist
with 3D CG elements by RACHEL ITO

New York

Nancy Drew Diaries
#2
"The Haunted Dollhouse" and "The Girl Who Wasn't There"
STEFAN PETRUCHA – Writer
SHO MURASE – Artist
with 3D CG elements by RACHEL ITO
BRYAN SENKA – Letterer
CARLOS JOSE GUZMAN
SHO MURASE
Colorists
MICHAEL PETRANEK – Associate Editor
JIM SALICRUP – Original Editor
BETH SCORZATO – Editor
JIM SALICRUP
Editor-in-Chief

ISBN: 978-1-59707-778-1

Published by arrangement with Aladdin Paperbacks,
an imprint of Simon & Schuster Children's Publishing Division.

Printed in South Korea
April 2016 by We SP Corp.
WE SP Co., Ltd
79-29 Soraji-ro, Paju-Si
Gyeonggi-do, Korea 10863

Distributed by Macmillian
Second Printing

NANCY DREW HERE. IT DOESN'T TAKE A DETECTIVE TO FIGURE OUT THAT YOU'RE PROBABLY WONDERING WHY I'M DRIVING THIS VINTAGE *ROADSTER* INSTEAD OF MY TRUSTY HYBRID.

WELL, MR. DAVE CRABTREE, AN ANTIQUE CAR DEALER, AND A CLIENT OF MY FATHER'S, *LOANED* IT TO ME. IN FACT, A FEW HOURS AGO HE LOANED OUT *ALL* HIS CARS.

NOPE, HE HASN'T GONE NUTS! IT'S ALL PART OF RIVER HEIGHTS *NOSTALGIA* WEEK!

EVERYONE PARTICIPATING (AND THAT'S MOST OF THE CITY!) IS WEARING 1930s CLOTHES AND USING PERIOD TECHNOLOGY TO CELEBRATE THE CREATION OF THE *STRATEMEYER FOUNDATION* IN 1930.

CHAPTER ONE: WHAT A DOLLHOUSE!

OUR HOUSEKEEPER, HANNAH, FOUND THE DREW FAMILY CONTRIBUTION, THIS ***OLD CLOCK*** UP IN THE ATTIC.

THE WEEK ENDS WITH AN ANTIQUE AUCTION – ALL THE ***PROCEEDS*** GOING TO THE FOUNDATION.

I WAS ON MY WAY TO DROP IT OFF AT CITY HALL AND WATCH THE OPENING CEREMONIES, LITTLE REALIZING A VINTAGE ***MYSTERY*** WAS ABOUT TO TAKE PLACE!

EVEN MY BEST PALS GEORGE AND BESS GOT INTO THE ACT.
ANTIQUES
SO, WHAT'S BUZZIN' COUSINS?
YIKES! CHECK OUT THOSE SPIFFY WHEELS!
HMM... BETTER GO EASY ON THE GAS, OR YOU COULD BLOW A BABBIT!
SOME PEOPLE WOULDN'T THINK A REAL DOLL, AS THEY USED TO SAY, LIKE BESS WOULD HAVE SUCH A KNACK WITH MACHINES, BUT SHE DOES!
OH, AND A BABBIT IS A SPECIAL ALLOY USED IN OLD CAR BEARINGS TO REDUCE THE FRICTION OF MOVING PARTS.

GREAT. NANCY GETS A TERRIFIC CAR, BUT I CAN'T EVEN USE MY CELL!
I CAN'T BELIEVE I LET YOU GUYS TALK ME INTO GIVING UP MY COMPUTER FOR A WHOLE WEEK! I MEAN, THAT'S LIKE ASKING NANCY TO GIVE UP MYSTERIES!
OH, YOU'RE JUST BEING A PARTY-POOPER!
I LOVE THIS OLD STUFF! THE 78 RPM RECORDS, THE OLD PHONES!
CAN YOU BELIEVE THEY USED TO MAKE RECORDINGS ON WIRES?
OKAY GALS, THIS THING IS HEAVY, SO WHAT SAY WE SHAKE A LEG AND GET OVER TO TOWN HALL?
SHAKE A WHAT?
1930s SLANG – IT MEANS LET'S GET GOING! SO LET'S!

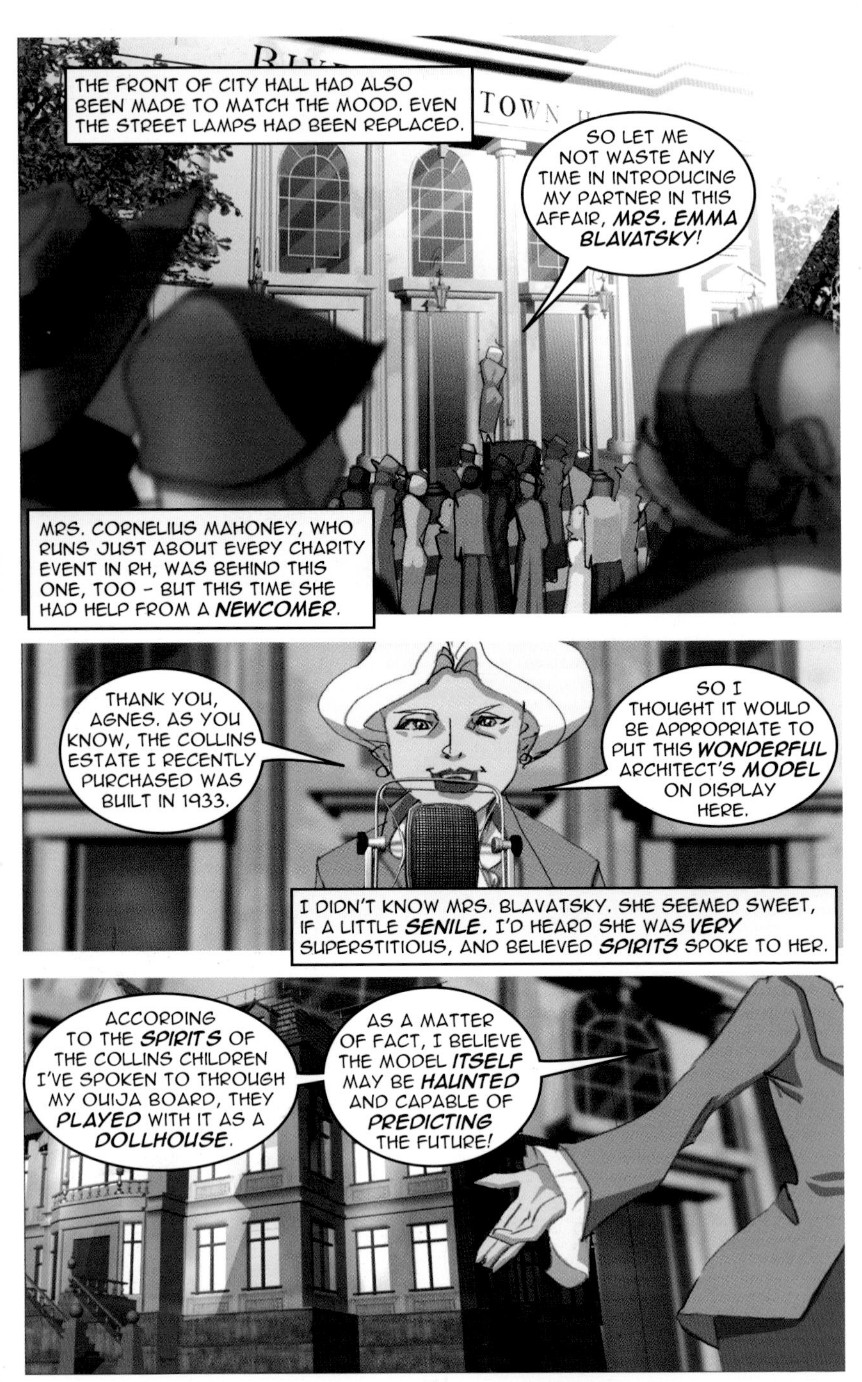
TOWN
THE FRONT OF CITY HALL HAD ALSO BEEN MADE TO MATCH THE MOOD. EVEN THE STREET LAMPS HAD BEEN REPLACED.
SO LET ME NOT WASTE ANY TIME IN INTRODUCING MY PARTNER IN THIS AFFAIR, MRS. EMMA BLAVATSKY!
MRS. CORNELIUS MAHONEY, WHO RUNS JUST ABOUT EVERY CHARITY EVENT IN RH, WAS BEHIND THIS ONE, TOO - BUT THIS TIME SHE HAD HELP FROM A NEWCOMER.
THANK YOU, AGNES. AS YOU KNOW, THE COLLINS ESTATE I RECENTLY PURCHASED WAS BUILT IN 1933.
SO I THOUGHT IT WOULD BE APPROPRIATE TO PUT THIS WONDERFUL ARCHITECT'S MODEL ON DISPLAY HERE.
I DIDN'T KNOW MRS. BLAVATSKY. SHE SEEMED SWEET, IF A LITTLE SENILE. I'D HEARD SHE WAS VERY SUPERSTITIOUS, AND BELIEVED SPIRITS SPOKE TO HER.
ACCORDING TO THE SPIRITS OF THE COLLINS CHILDREN I'VE SPOKEN TO THROUGH MY OUIJA BOARD, THEY PLAYED WITH IT AS A DOLLHOUSE.
AS A MATTER OF FACT, I BELIEVE THE MODEL ITSELF MAY BE HAUNTED AND CAPABLE OF PREDICTING THE FUTURE!

HAUNTED?! GIVE ME A BREAK! THE OLD DAME IS DYING FOR ATTENTION.
WELL... BUT... HOW DO YOU REALLY KNOW?
I THINK THIS CALLS FOR A CLOSER LOOK!
CHECK OUT THE DETAILS! IT'S EVEN GOT A LITTLE HIDDEN STAIRCASE!
WAIT A MINUTE.

WHY IS THAT DOLL WEARING A MASK, LIKE A BURGLAR? IT LOOKS AS THOUGH IT'S STEALING THE PAINTING. AND THAT WINDOW'S BROKEN!
SHEESH! I SWEAR YOU SEE A MYSTERY IN EVERYTHING, NANCE! IT'S BEEN A FEW DAYS SINCE YOUR LAST CASE, SO YOU'RE JUST GETTING ANTSY!

GEORGE WASN'T KIDDING, I DID HAVE A NOSE FOR MYSTERIES. BUT SHE, OF ALL PEOPLE, SHOULD KNOW MY HUNCHES USUALLY PAY OFF.
CRASH
AND THIS TIME, AGAIN, IT TURNED OUT, I WAS RIGHT.
ACCORDING TO THE POLICE REPORT, AT ABOUT THE SAME TIME WE WERE SPEAKING, THE SILENCE AT THE REAL BLAVATSKY HOME WAS SHATTERED BY THE SOUND OF BREAKING GLASS!
AND THE CRIME HAPPENED EXACTLY THE SAME WAY IT DID IN THE DOLL HOUSE!
CREEPY, HUH?
SO, DID THIS MEAN THE MODEL REALLY WAS HAUNTED?

I, FOR ONE, DON'T BELIEVE IN GHOSTS! IN MY EXPERIENCE, THERE'S ALWAYS A SIMPLE, REALISTIC EXPLANATION - EVEN WHEN IT LOOKS LIKE THERE ISN'T.
BUT IT CERTAINLY WAS A MYSTERY, WHICH MEANT NEXT MORNING, I HEADED STRAIGHT FOR THE CRIME SCENE!
I WAS A LITTLE SURPRISED TO SEE THAT EVEN THE RIVER HEIGHTS POLICE WERE USING OLD STYLE CARS!
THANKS TO THE CRACKED WINDOW WHERE THE BURGLAR ENTERED, I COULD CLEARLY HEAR CHIEF McGINNIS TALKING TO EMMA BLAVATSKY INSIDE.
SOMETIMES THE CHIEF FILLS ME IN ON DETAILS, SOMETIMES HE DOESN'T, SO I DECIDED TO EAVESDROP.
THAT'S THE PROOF IT WAS GHOSTS! THE PAINTING WAS WORTH-LESS!
MY BROTHER PAINTED IT AS A CHILD. FOR YEARS WE KEPT IT IN THE FAMILY BUNGALOW. IT WAS JUST LAST WEEK I TOOK IT OUT OF STORAGE!
FOR SOME REASON, THE SPIRITS ALWAYS WANTED IT!

I KNOW I SHOULDN'T *LAUGH* AT OTHER PEOPLE'S BELIEFS, BUT POOR MRS. BLAVATSKY JUST SOUNDED KIND OF *SILLY*!

THAT IS, UNTIL SHE REALLY STARTED *TALKING*...

I KNOW YOU THINK ME SENILE, CHIEF, BUT IS IT SO *HARD* TO BELIEVE *SOME* PART OF US SURVIVES *DEATH*? NEARLY *ALL* RELIGIONS DO!

EVERYONE HAS AT LEAST *ONE* STORY WHERE THEY'VE *SEEN* SOME-THING THEY CAN'T EXPLAIN, OR FELT THE *PRESENCE* OF A DEAR DEPARTED STANDING *NEAR*.

THE AIR IS FULL OF THE *ENERGIES* OF THOSE WHO WALKED THE EARTH BEFORE US. I *SPEAK* TO THEM, SOMETIMES *SEE* THEM, AND I *KNOW* THEY ARE IN THAT DOLLHOUSE.

WHY **NOT** BELIEVE THE VEIL BETWEEN OUR WORLDS SOMETIMES GROWS **THIN**, SOME LOST SOUL CAN SLIP THROUGH, AND THE **PAST** COME TO LIFE?

SHE SOUNDED SO SINCERE, SHE HAD **ME** WONDERING IF SOME GHOST MIGHT BE STANDING RIGHT NEXT TO ME!

BOO!
AHHHH!

HA-HA-HA-HA!
SORRY, NANCY, I SAW YOU OUT HERE A WHILE AGO AND, SINCE I ALREADY FEEL LIKE I'M DRESSED FOR HALLOWEEN, I COULDN'T RESIST GIVING YOU A LITTLE SCARE!

SINCE YOU'RE HERE, WHY DON'T YOU COME INSIDE? MRS. BLAVATSKY HAS ALREADY ASKED FOR YOU!
I WAS THINKING ABOUT MENTIONING HOW STRANGE HE LOOKED IN HIS OLD HAT, BUT DECIDED THAT I SHOULDN'T - ESPECIALLY SINCE HE WAS LETTING ME INTO THE CRIME SCENE!

HI, MRS. BLAVATSKY.
NANCY DREW! SO MANY PEOPLE RESPECT YOU IN RIVER HEIGHTS, PERHAPS YOU CAN CONVINCE THEM THAT THE SPIRITS ARE BEHIND THIS THEFT!
WELL, I'M AFRAID, FIRST I'D HAVE TO CONVINCE MYSELF!
AND I'D NEED TO KNOW WHY, FOR INSTANCE, A GHOST WOULD HAVE TO BREAK A WINDOW!
OR LEAVE FOOT-PRINTS!
POOR DEAR! SOME-TIMES YOU JUST HAVE TO STOP REASONING TO SEE THE TRUTH!

THE SPIRITS CONTROLLED WHOEVER BROKE IN HERE! THEY TOLD ME SO THEMSELVES!
IF THEY GAVE YOU HIS NAME, WE COULD FIND HIM AND RETURN THE PAINTING!
ALAS, THEY DO NOT SPEAK THAT CLEARLY, EVEN TO ME!
I SUGGEST YOU RETURN TO THE DOLLHOUSE! IT MAY HOLD THE ANSWERS FOR YOU!
HA! HOW ABOUT ALL THAT SPIRIT TALK! IT WAS PROBABLY JUST SOME PETTY THIEF WHO STOLE THE WRONG PAINTING!
IF YOU ASK ME, EMMA BLAVATSKY'S A SWEET OLD LOON!
I WOULDN'T INSULT OTHER PEOPLE'S TASTE IF I WERE WEARING THAT HAT, CHIEF McGINNIS!
VERY FUNNY, BUT SHE INSISTED! SHE DOESN'T WANT ANYTHING RUINING NOSTALGIA WEEK!

MUCH AS I AGREED WITH CHIEF McGINNIS, THAT STILL DIDN'T EXPLAIN THE DOLLHOUSE. IT'D BEEN MOVED INSIDE THE CITY HALL TO PROTECT IT FROM THE WEATHER.
HMM... EVERYONE WE ASKED SAID THE DOLLS WERE IN A DIFFERENT POSITION BEFORE THE UNVEILING! AND THE CASE WAS LOCKED THE WHOLE TIME!
WHAT KIND OF GHOST WOULD HAUNT A DOLLHOUSE, ANYWAY?
A LITTLE TINY GHOST?
MAKE FUN IF YOU LIKE, BUT THIS IS REALLY CREEPING ME OUT!
I HAVE A STUFFED MONKEY IN MY ROOM, A SOUVENIR FROM MY TRIP TO LILAC INN LAST SUMMER - AND NOW I CAN'T GET TO SLEEP BECAUSE I THINK IT'S STARING AT ME!
MAYBE YOU SHOULD COVER IT WITH A BLANKET.
BUT I'M AFRAID IT'LL SUFFO-CATE!
HEY! THAT SECURITY CAMERA WOULD SHOW WHATEVER HAPPENED TO THE DOLLHOUSE!

YEAH, CHIEF McGINNIS ALREADY ASKED ABOUT IT! SORRY, BUT THAT CAMERA'S ON THE *FRITZ*!
OH, WELL, I KIND OF FIGURED I SHOULD TRY TO SOLVE THIS CASE *WITHOUT* MODERN TECHNOLOGY, ANYWAY, IN KEEPING WITH THE... UH... *SPIRIT* OF NOSTALGIA WEEK!
OH, MY GOSH! OH, MY GOSH!
LOOK!
I TURNED MY BACK FOR A *SECOND* AND THE DOLLS *CHANGED*! I DIDN'T EVEN SEE THAT *TREE* BEFORE!
IT LOOKS LIKE THAT ONE IS STEALING A *HORSE*!

NOT ONLY THAT, BUT THE TOY TREE LOOKED JUST LIKE A PRETTY FAMOUS TREE RIGHT OUTSIDE RIVER HEIGHTS.

LEGEND HAD IT, THE RACKHAM GANG HAD A SHOOTOUT WITH A LOCAL FARMER HERE OVER A CENTURY AGO.

STRANGE SCENE FOR A NEW CRIME, BUT PERFECT FOR A PICNIC WITH MY BOYFRIEND, NED NICKERSON. AND AFTER TWO HOURS, NOT A HORSE IN SIGHT!

IT SAYS HERE SPIRITUALISM WAS BIG IN THE 1930s. PEOPLE USED EVERYTHING FROM AUTOMATIC WRITING TO TIPPING TABLES TO TALK TO THE DEAD!

YEAH, WELL, THE FAMOUS MAGICIAN HARRY HOUDINI SPENT A LOT OF HIS LIFE DEBUNKING THAT STUFF!
HE SWORE IF THERE WERE AN AFTERLIFE THAT HE'D COME BACK, AND WE'RE STILL WAITING!

MAYBE, BUT YOU HAVE TO ADMIT THERE ARE PROBABLY THINGS IN THE WORLD EVEN YOU CAN'T EXPLAIN!

NANCE?

NED WAS RIGHT, THERE WERE LOTS OF THINGS I COULDN'T EXPLAIN. AND RIGHT THEN, I WAS STARING AT ONE!

I DON'T BELIEVE IT! IT'S JUST LIKE THE DOLLHOUSE!
NOW THAT'S QUITE A COINCIDENCE!
DEIRDRE SHANNON? WHAT'RE YOU DOING ON A HORSE?
WELL, NOT EVERYONE RUSHED OFF TO SNATCH THE FREE CARS, AND MY FATHER THINKS IT WOULD LOOK BAD IF I VIOLATED NOSTALGIA WEEK!
BESIDES, RIDING'S MUCH MORE CLASSY THAN STEERING A FILTHY OLD TANK, DON'T YOU THINK? DADDY RENTED ME THIS WONDERFUL GIRL FROM SHADOW RANCH.
DEIRDRE'S BEEN MY NEMESIS SINCE GRADE SCHOOL. BUT SOMETIMES IT FEELS LIKE SHE'S BEEN TRYING TO GET THE BEST OF ME SINCE THE 1930s!
TO MAKE THINGS WORSE, SHE'S ALWAYS TRYING TO FLIRT WITH MY BOYFRIEND!
NED, YOU SURE ARE THE BEE'S FLEAS IN THAT OUTFIT!
IF YOU MEAN THE OLD SLANG TERM, I THINK YOU MEAN BEE'S KNEES! BUT THANKS, I THINK...

LOOK, DIERDRE, THE FIGURES IN MADAME BLAVATSKY'S DOLLHOUSE AT THE TOWN CENTER SHOWED SOMEONE STEALING A HORSE RIGHT BY THIS TREE.
THE LAST CRIME IT SHOWED CAME TRUE! SO... I KNOW IT SOUNDS WEIRD, BUT I THINK YOU SHOULD BE CAREFUL!
SOUNDS WEIRD?! HMM... NOW WHY WOULD IT SOUND WEIRD?
OH, I KNOW! THAT'S BECAUSE IT IS WEIRD! TOTALLY WEIRD! JUST LIKE THOSE CLOTHES YOU HAVE ON!
OH, DEAR! I'D BETTER GET HOME AND CONSULT MY MONOPOLY BOARD TO PROTECT MYSELF!
SO NED, WANT TO COME WITH?
I THINK YOU MEANT OUIJA BOARD, AND, NO THANKS!

HAVE IT YOUR WAY! GUESS I'D BETTER GET OUT OF HERE BEFORE SOME HORSE THIEVES SHOW UP!
HA! THAT'S MORE WILD WEST THAN 1930s ANYWAY!
UH... DEIRDRE?
LOOK OUT!
NED, HELP!

WHOA! EASY THERE!
DISTRACT HIM! I'LL GET THE HORSE!
DISTRACT HIM?
LIKE THIS?
WOK
I FIGURED THERE MUST BE SOMETHING SPECIAL ABOUT THE HORSE IF THE CROOK WANTED IT SO BADLY!

AND I WASN'T ABOUT TO LET A BIG CLUE LIKE THAT SLIP AWAY!
UNFORTUNATELY, THOUGH NED'S PRETTY STRONG, THE CROOK SLIPPED AWAY FROM HIM!
AND I HAD A FEELING AN APPLE WASN'T GOING TO STOP HIM THIS TIME!
ESPECIALLY WHEN HE HAD A TRUCK!
OF COURSE IN KEEPING WITH NOSTALGIA WEEK, I DIDN'T BRING MY CELL! AND THE CLOSEST PLACE TO GO FOR HELP WAS RED GATE FARM, FIVE MILES AWAY!
NED HOPPED IN MY ROADSTER TO HELP, BUT IT WASN'T MADE FOR OFF-ROAD DRIVING!

NOT ONLY WAS THE CHASE OFF-ROAD, BUT SOON, I WAS OFF-HORSE!
UNLIKE DEIRDRE, I WASN'T EXACTLY DRESSED FOR RIDING, Y'KNOW.
MY HEAD HIT SOME-THING, HARD.
I FELT GRASS UNDER ME, THEN EVERYTHING STARTED GOING FUZZY.
THE LAST THING I REMEMBERED WAS THE CROOK TAKING THE HORSE BACK TOWARD HIS TRUCK.
THEN-- FOR THE LONGEST TIME NOTHING.

NEXT THING I KNEW, I WAS IN A BALLROOM. EVERYONE I KNEW WAS THERE, ONLY THEY ALL WORE OLD STYLE CLOTHES. IT WAS SOME KIND OF PARTY.
NED AND I WHIRLED ACROSS THE FLOOR.
SO I KNEW IT WAS A DREAM. I LOVE NED, HE'S GREAT, BUT HE'S NOT MUCH OF A DANCER.
THEN HE SAID SOMETHING TERRIBLY FUNNY, OR I GUESS HE DID, BECAUSE WE WERE BOTH LAUGHING.
IT WAS THE PERFECT EVENING, THE PERFECT DATE, THE PERFECT DREAM...

ONLY, IT TURNS OUT, IT WASN'T A DREAM.
IT WAS A NIGHTMARE!
NOW DO YOU BELIEVE SPIRITS HAUNT MY DOLLHOUSE?

YEOW!
WELCOME BACK TO THE WORLD OF THE LIVING!
TO ANSWER YOUR FIRST QUESTION, NED IS FINE. HE'S DOWNSTAIRS, WAITING.
TO ANSWER YOUR NEXT TWO QUESTIONS, NO, THEY DIDN'T CATCH THE CROOK AND YOU'VE BEEN OUT FOR ABOUT THREE HOURS.
HANNAH'S BEEN OUR HOUSEKEEPER EVER SINCE MOM DIED WHEN I WAS LITTLE. SOMETIMES I THINK SHE KNOWS ME BETTER THAN I KNOW MYSELF.
AND THE DOCTOR SAYS YOU'LL BE FINE, TOO. DID I LEAVE ANYTHING OUT?
NOPE! I GUESS THAT COVERS IT!

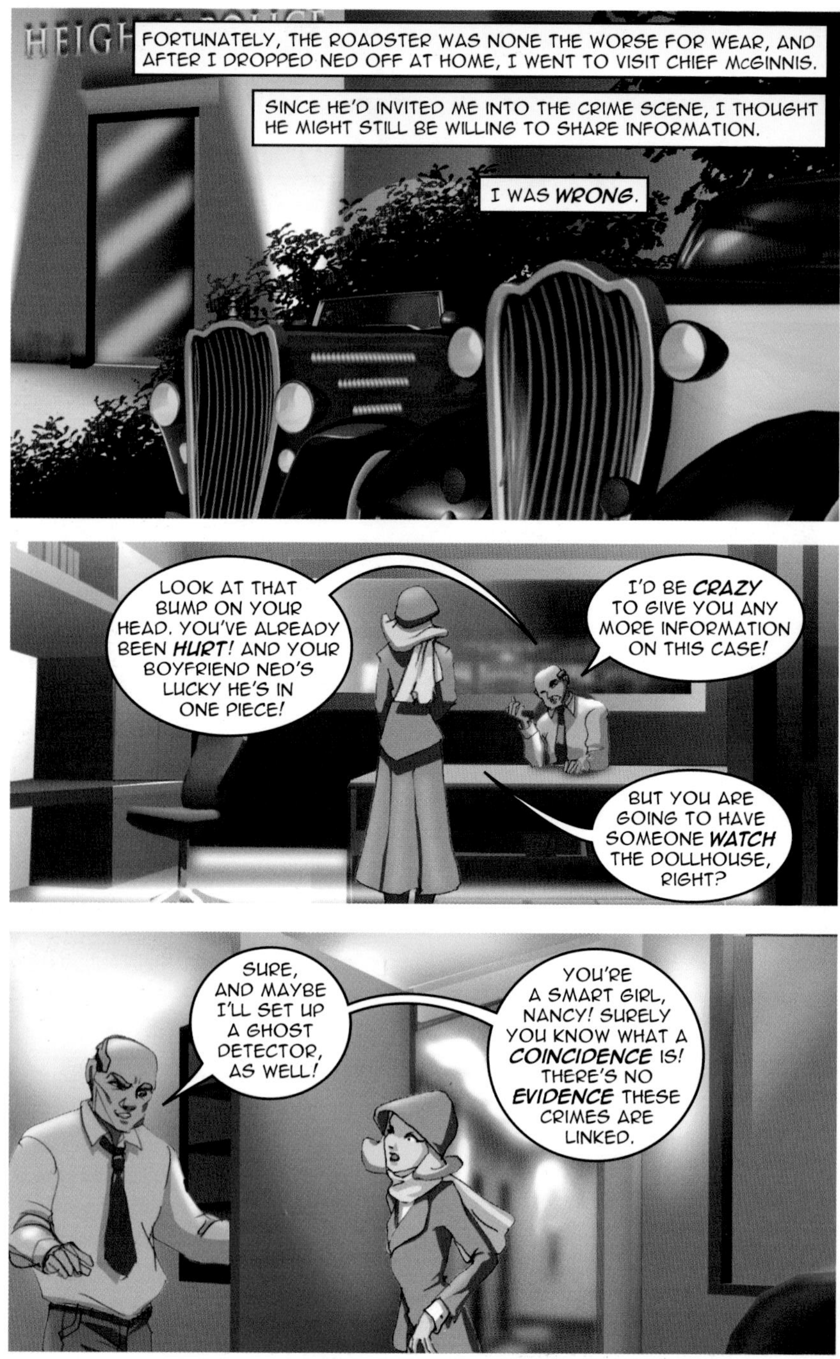
FORTUNATELY, THE ROADSTER WAS NONE THE WORSE FOR WEAR, AND AFTER I DROPPED NED OFF AT HOME, I WENT TO VISIT CHIEF McGINNIS.
SINCE HE'D INVITED ME INTO THE CRIME SCENE, I THOUGHT HE MIGHT STILL BE WILLING TO SHARE INFORMATION.
I WAS WRONG.
I'D BE CRAZY TO GIVE YOU ANY MORE INFORMATION ON THIS CASE!
LOOK AT THAT BUMP ON YOUR HEAD. YOU'VE ALREADY BEEN HURT! AND YOUR BOYFRIEND NED'S LUCKY HE'S IN ONE PIECE!
BUT YOU ARE GOING TO HAVE SOMEONE WATCH THE DOLLHOUSE, RIGHT?
SURE, AND MAYBE I'LL SET UP A GHOST DETECTOR, AS WELL!
YOU'RE A SMART GIRL, NANCY! SURELY YOU KNOW WHAT A COINCIDENCE IS! THERE'S NO EVIDENCE THESE CRIMES ARE LINKED.

TECHNICALLY, HE WAS RIGHT I SUPPOSE, BUT I HAD A HUNCH, AND MY HUNCHES ARE SELDOM WRONG.
SO, IF CHIEF McGINNIS WASN'T GOING TO DO A STAKEOUT ON THE DOLLHOUSE...
THEN I WOULD.
SOMEONE HAD TO BE MOVING THOSE DOLLS AROUND, AND TO FIND OUT WHO, I DECIDED TO DO IT THE OLD FASHIONED WAY...
BY SITTING AND WATCHING.
UNFORTUNATELY, THIS MEANT A LITTLE BREAKING AND ENTERING, BUT IT WAS FOR A GOOD CAUSE.

BESS AND GEORGE THINK THAT WHEN I HAVE MY HEAD IN A MYSTERY, I FORGET EVERYTHING ELSE - GAS, APPOINTMENTS...
THEY EVEN THINK I FORGET TO BE SCARED.
THEY'RE WRONG ABOUT THAT PART. I CERTAINLY DO GET SCARED, PARTICULARLY WHEN I'M ALL ALONE AT NIGHT IN A HUGE BUILDING.
FOCUSING HELPS, THINKING ABOUT THE PROBLEM. THEN, BEFORE YOU KNOW IT...
HOURS PASS.

FINALLY, AT ABOUT THREE IN THE MORNING, I HEARD SOMETHING.
A QUICK SHINE OF THE FLASHLIGHT SHOWED A MOVING SHADOW.
SKRCH SKRCH
I KNOW IT WAS RIDICULOUS, BUT PART OF ME WAS HALF-EXPECTING TO SEE ONE OF MRS. BLAVATSKY'S SPIRITS.
I SHOOK THE THOUGHT OUT OF MY HEAD, AND TRIED TO FOCUS, TO QUIET MY BEATING HEART.
SKRCH SKRCH
BUT NOTHING COULD HAVE PREPARED ME FOR WHAT I SAW...
SKRCH SKRCH

THE DOLLS WERE MOVING BY *THEMSELVES!*
END CHAPTER ONE

I'D LIKE TO SAY I WASN'T SCARED, BUT COME ON, THE DOLLS WERE MOVING!
I MEAN, I'M USUALLY PRETTY GOOD ABOUT THIS KIND OF THING, BUT YES, I WAS OFFICIALLY FREAKED.
I WANTED TO RUN, BUT MY FEET WOULDN'T COOPERATE.
IN A WAY, IT MAY HAVE BEEN LUCKY I FELL, BECAUSE BY THE TIME I GOT BACK UP, I'D GOTTEN A HOLD OF MYSELF.
OOPS!
I REALIZED THAT SINCE IT COULDN'T BE SPIRITS, IT MUST BE SOME SORT OF TRICK, AND I WAS DETERMINED TO FIND OUT WHAT KIND OF TRICK IT WAS!
CHAPTER TWO: GHOST OF A CLUE

BUT BEFORE I COULD GET BACK TO THE DOLLHOUSE...
SOMEONE IN THERE?
MR. DUNCAN, THE WATCHMAN, LOOKED SO MUCH LIKE HE'D STEPPED FROM THE PAST, IT WAS HARD NOT TO SMILE.
DON'T BE LOOKING AT ME FUNNY, NANCY DREW, I'M NOT THE ONE TRES-PASSING!
MAYOR STRONG ASKED ME TO WEAR THIS GET-UP FOR NOSTALGIA WEEK! WHAT'S YOUR EXCUSE?
WHEN I EXPLAINED HE HURRIED OVER TO THE HOUSE.
DAGNAB IT! CHIEF McGINNIS TOLD ME TO KEEP AN EYE OUT. NOW I'VE MISSED THE WHOLE THING!
THE DOLLS REALLY DID CHANGE! THIS IS ONE FOR THE OL' DIARY! IF I HAD A CLUE WHERE I PUT IT, THAT IS!

MR. DUNCAN, DID YOU SEE THIS DOLLHOUSE SET UP? COULD THE DOLLS BE MECHANICAL? WAS THERE ANY MACHINERY?
DON'T THINK SO. I THINK IT WAS SOLID.
EXCUSE ME.
SURE THING.
I FIGURED THERE WAS ONLY ONE WAY TO SOLVE THIS MYSTERY FOR SURE!
HEY! THAT'S PRIVATE PROPERTY!

MRS. BLAVATSKY WOULD SCREAM BLOODY MURDER IF YOU SMASHED HER OLD DOLL-HOUSE!
ACTUALLY, I WAS JUST AIMING TO CRACK THE CASE, BUT HE WAS RIGHT. SOMETIMES I JUST GET SO FOCUSED ON A MYSTERY, I FORGET MYSELF A LITTLE.
WHAT'S THAT?
THE POLICE. I CALLED SOON AS I HEARD SOMETHING MOVING IN HERE, JUST LIKE I WAS SUPPOSED TO!
GREAT. I FIGURED I'D BE ARRESTED FOR TRESPASSING! I WONDERED WHAT 1930s PRISONS LOOKED LIKE.
AS IT TURNED OUT, CHIEF McGINNIS WASN'T AS ANGRY AS I EXPECTED. BUT HE DIDN'T EXACTLY BELIEVE ME, EITHER.
IT'S LATE, YOU'RE TIRED AND YOU HAD THAT BUMP ON YOUR HEAD. SURE YOU JUST DIDN'T IMAGINE IT?
TELL YOU THE TRUTH, NANCY, I WANTED TO CRACK OPEN THAT CASE MYSELF AFTER THE HORSE THEFT.
BUT MRS. BLAVATSKY REFUSED. I EVEN TRIED TO CONVINCE JUDGE WATERS TO GIVE ME A WARRANT, BUT HE DOESN'T LOOK KINDLY ON GHOST STORIES!
AND WITH THAT NEW DEAD END, IT WAS TIME FOR THIS GIRL DETECTIVE TO GET SOME SLEEP.

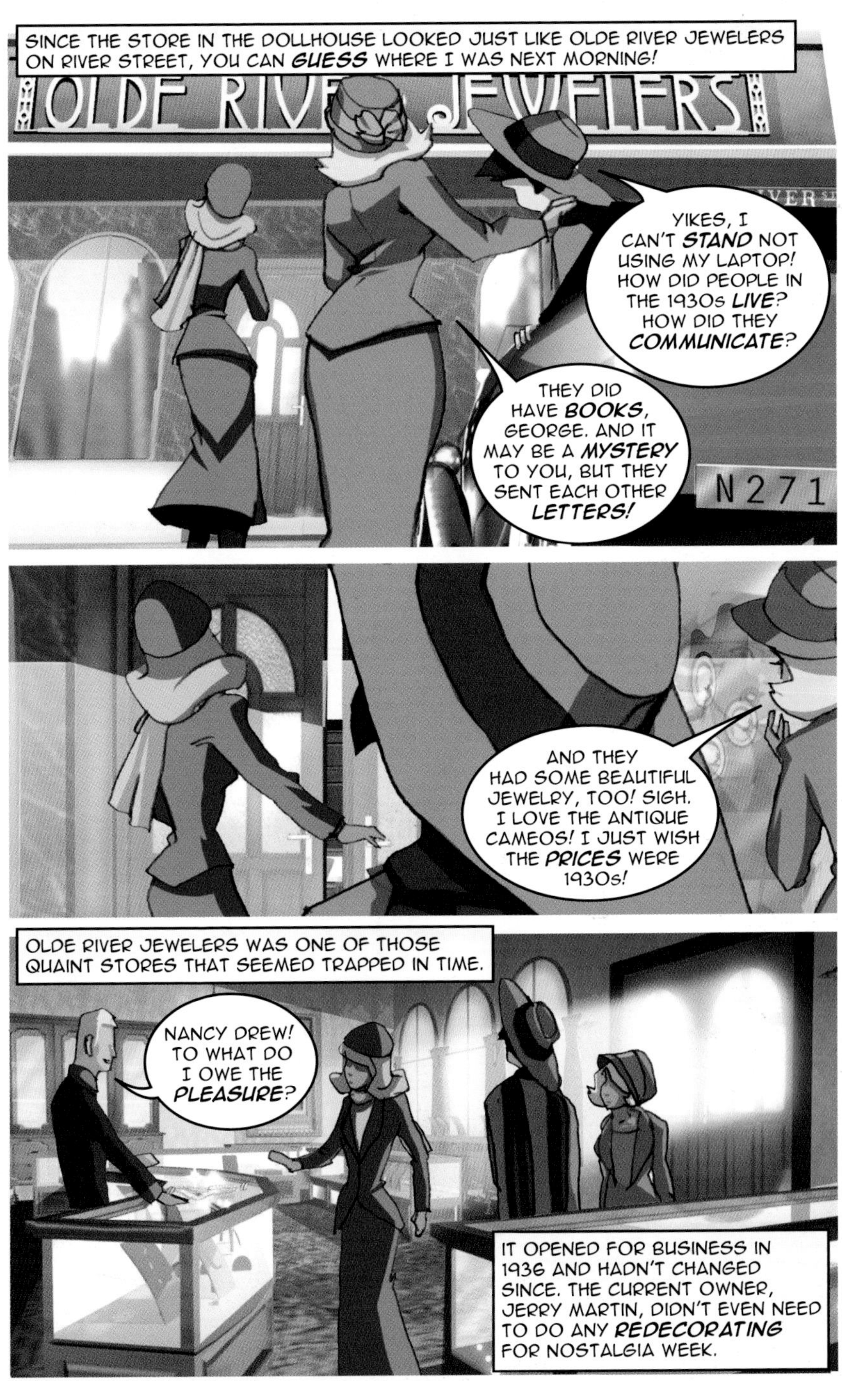
SINCE THE STORE IN THE DOLLHOUSE LOOKED JUST LIKE OLDE RIVER JEWELERS ON RIVER STREET, YOU CAN GUESS WHERE I WAS NEXT MORNING!
OLDE RIVE JEWELERS
YIKES, I CAN'T STAND NOT USING MY LAPTOP! HOW DID PEOPLE IN THE 1930s LIVE? HOW DID THEY COMMUNICATE?
THEY DID HAVE BOOKS, GEORGE. AND IT MAY BE A MYSTERY TO YOU, BUT THEY SENT EACH OTHER LETTERS!
N271
AND THEY HAD SOME BEAUTIFUL JEWELRY, TOO! SIGH. I LOVE THE ANTIQUE CAMEOS! I JUST WISH THE PRICES WERE 1930s!
OLDE RIVER JEWELERS WAS ONE OF THOSE QUAINT STORES THAT SEEMED TRAPPED IN TIME.
NANCY DREW! TO WHAT DO I OWE THE PLEASURE?
IT OPENED FOR BUSINESS IN 1936 AND HADN'T CHANGED SINCE. THE CURRENT OWNER, JERRY MARTIN, DIDN'T EVEN NEED TO DO ANY REDECORATING FOR NOSTALGIA WEEK.

I FEEL A LITTLE SILLY SAYING THIS, BUT DID CHIEF McGINNIS TELL YOU ABOUT THE UH... DOLLHOUSE, MR. MARTIN?
THAT HE DID! HE'S STOPPING BY HIMSELF EVERY HOUR. NOSTALGIA WEEK HAS THE RIVER HEIGHTS POLICE DEPARTMENT STRETCHED PRETTY THIN, I GUESS.
YOU'RE NOT WORRIED?
ABOUT A HAUNTED DOLLHOUSE? I THOUGHT IT WAS PRETTY FUNNY!
THAT KIND OF STUFF MAY HAVE BEEN SPOOKY A LONG TIME AGO! BUT, THIS ISN'T REALLY THE 1930s!
I MEAN, DO YOU EXPECT ME TO BELIEVE SOMEONE WITH A MASK WILL JUST WALK IN HERE AND SAY...

OKAY! THAT NECKLACE WILL DO ***NICELY***!

AND DON'T GET ANY FUNNY IDEAS ABOUT FOLLOWING ME, ESPECIALLY YOU, NANCY DREW!
THE SPIRITS WOULDN'T LIKE THAT!
WHOA, GIRL! YOU STAY RIGHT HERE!
I'M NOT AFRAID OF ANY SPIRITS!
FORGET THE SPIRITS, DIDN'T YOU SEE THE GUN?

THEY MADE ME COUNT TO TEN, THEN AGREED TO LET ME SEE IF I COULD FIGURE OUT WHICH DIRECTION HE RAN IN.
HE VANISHED! LIKE A... GHOST!
NO, LIKE SOME-ONE WITH A CAR.
THOSE TIRE TRACKS ARE FRESH.
I THOUGHT ABOUT FOLLOWING WITH MY CAR, BUT THE CROOK WAS LONG GONE.
STRANGER STILL, I SOON LEARNED THAT THE STOLEN NECKLACE WAS FAKE! MR. MARTIN JUST USED IT FOR DISPLAY!

DID YOU KNOW IN 1924, AMERICANS CONSUMED LESS THAN 4 QUARTS OF ICE CREAM A YEAR? TODAY, IT'S LIKE 15 QUARTS.
THAT WAS THE LAST THING I READ ON THE INTERNET. I MISS IT SO MUCH!
THIS IS A TOUGH ONE! WHAT MADE THOSE DOLLS MOVE? AND WHY STEAL A FAKE PAINTING... A FAKE NECKLACE?
MAYBE SINCE THE SPIRIT DOLLS ARE LITTLE FAKE PEOPLE, THEY LIKE FAKE STUFF!
WILL YOU STOP WITH THE SPIRIT STUFF, BESS? DEIRDRE'S HORSE WAS REAL. AT LEAST IT LOOKED REAL.
OW! YOU'RE MEAN IN THE 1930s!
OH, SHE'S JUST GRUMPY WITHOUT HER MODERN CON-VENIENCES.
THE HORSE WAS REAL, JUST NOT VALUABLE! MAYBE THAT'S THE POINT. MAYBE THE CROOK ISN'T STEALING STUFF TO MAKE MONEY.
WHY ELSE WOULD SOMEONE STEAL? IT'S A LOUSY WAY TO GET FAMOUS!

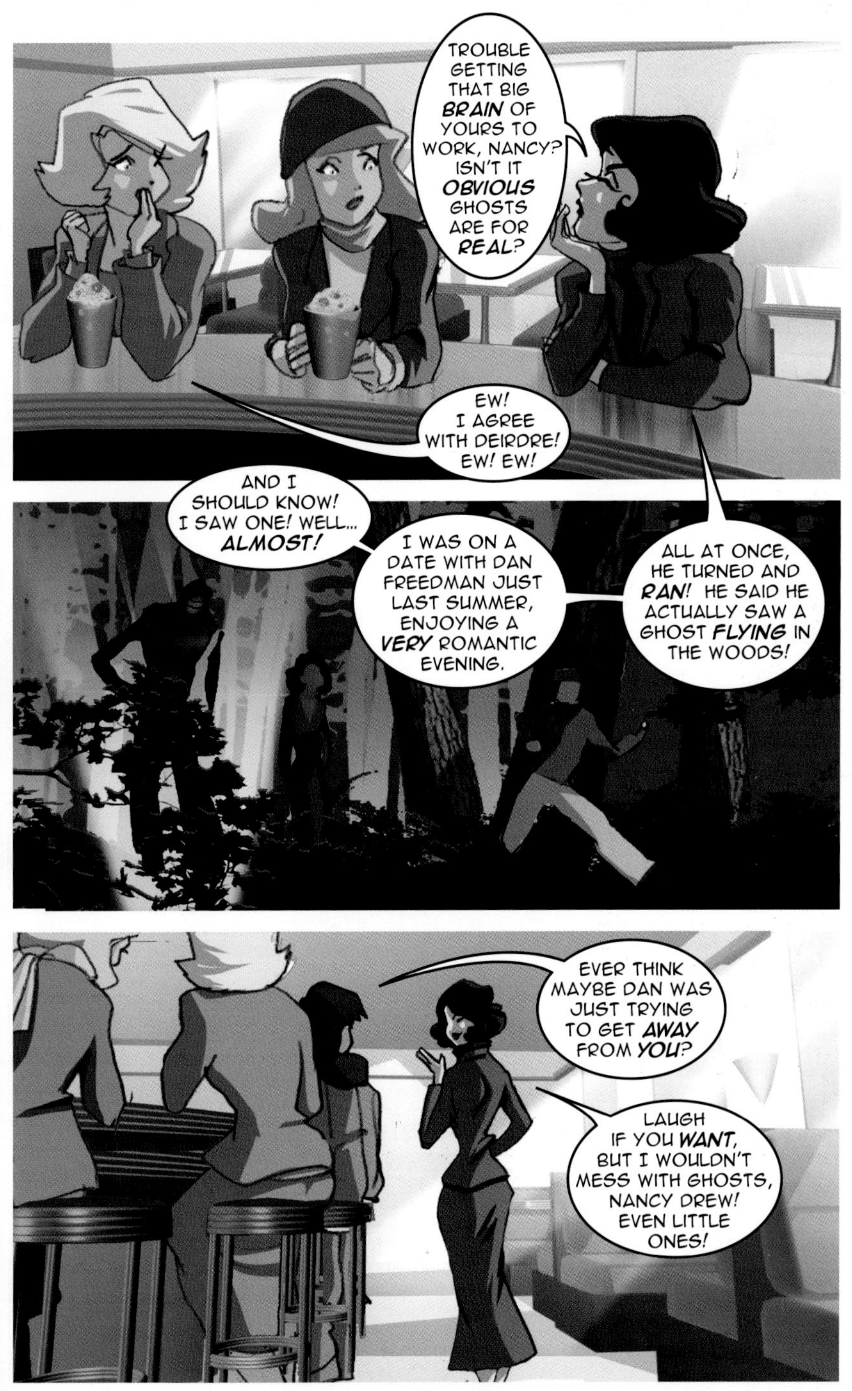
TROUBLE GETTING THAT BIG BRAIN OF YOURS TO WORK, NANCY? ISN'T IT OBVIOUS GHOSTS ARE FOR REAL?
EW! I AGREE WITH DEIRDRE! EW! EW!
AND I SHOULD KNOW! I SAW ONE! WELL... ALMOST!
I WAS ON A DATE WITH DAN FREEDMAN JUST LAST SUMMER, ENJOYING A VERY ROMANTIC EVENING.
ALL AT ONCE, HE TURNED AND RAN! HE SAID HE ACTUALLY SAW A GHOST FLYING IN THE WOODS!
EVER THINK MAYBE DAN WAS JUST TRYING TO GET AWAY FROM YOU?
LAUGH IF YOU WANT, BUT I WOULDN'T MESS WITH GHOSTS, NANCY DREW! EVEN LITTLE ONES!

STEAMBOATS ACTUALLY GO ALL THE WAY BACK TO 1769, BUT THEY DIDN'T MAKE MUCH MONEY UNTIL ROBERT FULTON STARTED BUILDING THEM IN 1801.

TECHNICALLY THE MAGNOLIA BELLE WAS A LOT OLDER THAN 1930, BUT IT WAS LAST FIXED UP IN 1935, SO IT FIT RIGHT IN!

GOOD THING, TOO - SHE WAS A GLORIOUS OLD SHIP!

EVEN MY DAD, CARSON DREW, WAS THERE, DOING THE LINDY WITH MRS. MAHONEY. HE'S A GREAT LAWYER, AND NOT A BAD DANCER!
THE "LINDY HOP" WAS NAMED AFTER CHARLES LINDBERGH, THE FIRST MAN TO "HOP" ACROSS THE ATLANTIC OCEAN IN A SOLO FLIGHT IN 1927. THE DANCE WAS A HUGE CRAZE BY THE 1930s
SHALL WE CUT A RUG? THAT'S OLD SLANG FOR...
I KNOW, NED, FOR DANCING. SURE!
FUNNY, BUT LINDBERGH NEVER DANCED HIMSELF. AND BY THE LATE 1930S, THE NAME OF THE DANCE CHANGED TO THE JITTERBUG ANYWAY!
WHATEVER THE NAME, IT SURE WAS A LOT OF FUN!

I WAS HAVING A GREAT TIME, BUT MY MIND KEPT DRIFTING BACK TO OTHER THINGS.
THINGS LIKE, WAS I WRONG? WAS I BEING TOO SKEPTICAL ABOUT THE SPIRIT WORLD?
THERE WAS A KIND OF MAGIC FEELING IN THE AIR AS WE REACHED OUT TO THE PAST.
SO, WAS IT IMPOSSIBLE TO THINK THAT THE PAST COULD ALSO BE REACHING OUT TO US?

YOU KNOW, BACK IN THE REAL 1930s, THERE PROBABLY WEREN'T ANY GIRL DETECTIVES!
EMMA BLAVATSKY!

ACTUALLY, ANNE RODWAY SOLVED THE MURDER OF HER BEST FRIEND BACK IN 1859. I THINK SHE WAS THE FIRST.
MRS. BLAVATSKY, IF YOU DON'T MIND MY ASKING, WHY WON'T YOU LET US OPEN THE DOLLHOUSE? DO YOU HAVE SOMETHING TO HIDE?
HIDE? AT MY AGE, THERE IS LITTLE TO HIDE.
I DON'T WISH THE HOUSE DISTURBED, BECAUSE IT WOULD DISTURB THE SPIRITS! THEY HAVE SO MUCH TO TELL US.
THEY SURE HAVE AN ODD WAY OF TALKING! PREDICTING THE THEFT OF WORTHLESS THINGS?
YOU DOUBT, BUT WHAT IF YOUR CLUES LED TO PROOF THAT THE SPIRIT WORLD REALLY DOES EXIST?
PROOF? WELL, I GUESS I'D BE PRETTY FAMOUS THEN, WOULDN'T I?
WHY DON'T YOU COME TO MY HOME TOMORROW, AND TOGETHER WE CAN TRY TO CONTACT THEM?
WHO KNOWS? PERHAPS WE WILL BOTH BE FAMOUS.

I CAN'T BELIEVE I LET YOU GUYS TALK ME INTO A SEANCE!
COME ON, YOU KNOW YOU'RE DYING TO SEE A GHOSTY!
IT'S THE DYING PART THAT SCARES ME!

YOU'RE ALL HERE. EXCELLENT. LET'S GET STARTED!
IN THERE? IN THE DARK?

THE SPIRITS PREFER THE DARK, MY DEAR. THEIR DAYS IN THE LIGHT ARE OVER, AND IT MAKES THEM FEEL AT HOME.

DARKNESS ALSO MAKES IT EASIER TO FOOL PEOPLE!

I KIND OF KNEW WHAT TO EXPECT.
PLEASE. BE SEATED.
SEE, AFTER THE DANCE, NED LOANED ME THE BOOK HE WAS READING ABOUT SPIRITUALISM.

GOOD THING, TOO, OR I MIGHT HAVE BEEN FOOLED.
THIS TWISTED CANDLE HAS BEEN SPECIALLY BLESSED TO ATTRACT SPIRITS!
BUT AS IT TURNED OUT, EMMA BLAVATSKY WENT TOTALLY BY THE BOOK!
FIRST, WE WERE ASKED TO HOLD HANDS.
LETS US JOIN TOGETHER IN A CIRCLE, AND LET THIS CIRCLE REMAIN UNBROKEN.
THEN, MRS. BLAVATSKY, WHO ACTED AS OUR "MEDIUM" SAID A FEW WORDS TO INVOKE THE DEAD.
HEAR ME, SPIRITS OF THE DEPARTED! I KNOW YOU WALK AMONG US! I KNOW YOU WATCH US AND CRAVE TO SPEAK!
PLEASE TELL US! TELL IS WHAT YOU WANT US TO KNOW!

FOR A WHILE, NOTHING HAPPENED.
THEN, ALL AT ONCE, I FELT LIKE MY HAND WAS BEING SQUEEZED IN A VISE!
THEN I REALIZED IT WAS BESS! THE POOR DEAR WAS SO SCARED SHE WAS CRUSHING MY HAND.
RELAX. IT HASN'T EVEN STARTED YET.
Y-YES IT HAS, N-N-NANCE! LOOK!

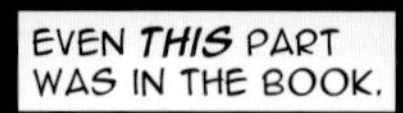
EVEN *THIS* PART WAS IN THE BOOK.

SPIRITUALISTS CLAIMED THESE GHOSTLY FORMS WERE MADE FROM SOMETHING CALLED ***ECTOPLASM.***

BUT IT WAS REALLY USUALLY ***MUSLIN***, A CHEAP FABRIC THAT COULD BE ROLLED UP AND EASILY HIDDEN.

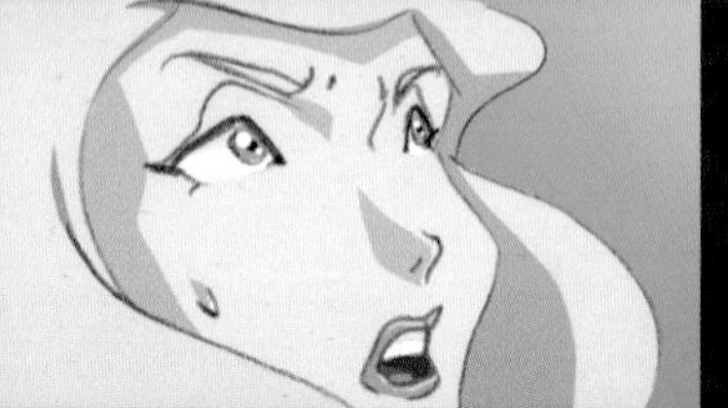

PRETTY ***IMPRESSIVE***, THOUGH, HUH?

OHHHHHH!
AT THE HEIGHT OF THE SEANCE, THE SPIRIT WOULD ALWAYS FIND SOME WAY TO COMMUNICATE.
SOMETIMES THEY TAPPED OUT ANSWERS TO QUESTIONS BY TIPPING THE TABLE.
SOMETIMES THEY MOVED A PEN IN THE HAND OF THE MEDIUM TO WRITE A MESSAGE.
AND SOMETIMES, THEY USED THE MOUTH OF THE MEDIUM TO JUST, WELL... TALK!
OHHHHHH!
DO NOT DOUBT US NANCY DREW! TELL THE WORLD WE ARE REAL!
OR YOU WILL BECOME A VICTIM OF OUR CURSE!
AND, OF COURSE, AT THE VERY END, THE CANDLE ALWAYS GETS MYSTERIOUSLY BLOWN OUT!
WHOOSH

THEN THE MEDIUM WAKES UP AND ACTS LIKE NOTHING HAPPENED!
MY, MY!
THE REALLY AMAZING THING IS HOW MANY PEOPLE BELIEVED THIS STUFF!
I MUST HAVE PASSED OUT FROM THE EXCITEMENT!
SO, DID ANYTHING HAPPEN? DID THE SPIRITS SPEAK?
DID ANYTHING HAPPEN?!
DID ANYTHING HAPPEN?!
THERE WAS A BIG GHOST AND... AND...A WEIRD VOICE AND IT THREATENED NANCY!

BESS, THERE'S A BOOK YOU'VE REALLY GOT TO READ! IT EXPLAINS HOW ALL THESE SEANCES ARE FAKED.
FAKED?
YEAH, LIKE NOT REAL! SOME PEOPLE PAY A MINT TO SPEAK TO THEIR DEAD LOVED ONES! GEE, FOR A MECHANICAL GENIUS, YOU SURE CAN BE GULLIBLE!
GEORGE IS A LITTLE CRANKY, BUT SHE'S RIGHT.
THEY USED ALL KINDS OF TRICKS, LIKE WIRES, FOLDS IN THEIR CLOTHING, HOLLOW SPACES IN THE TABLE--
WAIT A MINUTE--

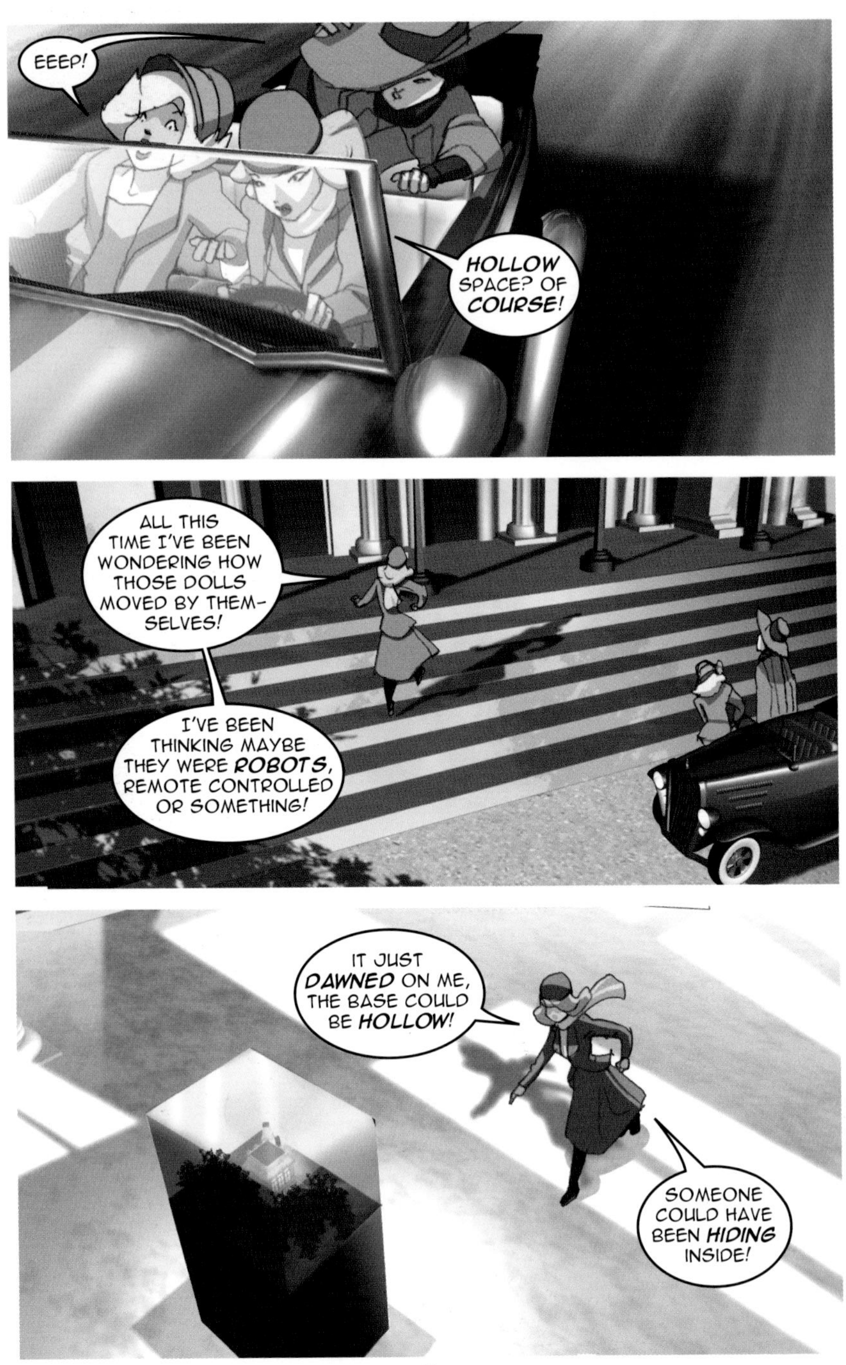
EEEP!
HOLLOW SPACE? OF COURSE!
ALL THIS TIME I'VE BEEN WONDERING HOW THOSE DOLLS MOVED BY THEM-SELVES!
I'VE BEEN THINKING MAYBE THEY WERE ROBOTS, REMOTE CONTROLLED OR SOMETHING!
IT JUST DAWNED ON ME, THE BASE COULD BE HOLLOW!
SOMEONE COULD HAVE BEEN HIDING INSIDE!

BUT THAT DOESN'T EXPLAIN HOW THE DOLLS *MOVED!*
NO, BUT *MAGNETS* WOULD!
IF THERE WERE *MAGNETS* IN THE DOLLS, SOMEONE COULD MOVE THEM FROM BENEATH WITH *ANOTHER* MAGNET.
HMM... THIS ALL LOOKS *SOLID*.
WAIT! THERE'S SOMETHING WEDGED UNDER IT!

PUSH, GIRLS, PUSH!
UNGH! EASY FOR YOU TO SAY!
THIS IS HEAVY FOR A HAUNTED DOLLHOUSE.
OOOMF! GOT IT!
WHAT IS IT?
SOME KIND OF BROKEN LOCKET!

YOU HERE AGAIN, NANCY?
CHIEF McGINNIS! WE'VE GOT TO GET THIS BASE OPEN!
SORRY, NANCY, SAME PROBLEM AS THE HOUSE! IT BELONGS TO MRS. BLAVATSKY!
FUNNY THOUGH, YOU WERE SO CONCERNED WITH THE BASE, YOU DIDN'T NOTICE WHAT ELSE HAD CHANGED!
YIKES, THIS TIME THE DOLLS DIDN'T JUST CHANGE, THE WHOLE HOUSE DID!
IT LOOKS LIKE THE OLD MANSION ON LARKSPUR LANE!
WHAT'S THE CRIME THIS TIME?
MURDER.
THAT DOLL ON THE ROOF PUSHED THAT OTHER DOLL OFF.

NANCY, I HATE TO SAY IT, BUT THAT DOLL LYING THERE ON THE GROUND, KIND OF DEAD?
IT LOOKS LIKE YOU! IT'S EVEN GOT A LITTLE LOCKET IN ITS HAND!
AND THE CAR PARKED OUT FRONT LOOKS LIKE YOURS!
N2701
COME ON, HOW DO YOU KNOW IT'S NOT JUST ANY OLD BLUE ROADSTER?
ULP!
BECAUSE THE LICENSE PLATE IS THE SAME AS MINE!
N2701
END CHAPTER TWO

WON'T YOU PLEASE LET ME HELP LOOK FOR CLUES, CHIEF McGINNIS?
SORRY, BUT NO! CITY HALL IS OFFICIALLY CLOSED UNTIL WE GET TO THE BOTTOM OF THIS, AND I PROMISED YOUR FATHER I'D SEND YOU HOME!
WHATEVER YOU DO, DO NOT HEAD TO LARKSPUR LANE!
THAT PLACE IS FALLING APART! IT'S DANGEROUS WHETHER SOMETHING FISHY IS GOING ON OR NOT! LET THE POLICE HANDLE THINGS FOR A CHANGE!

CHAPTER THREE: NANCY GETS DOLLED UP

EEEP! I'M SO FREAKED OUT, I THOUGHT I HEARD THAT STATUE WHISPER!
THE ONLY WAY THAT STATUE COULD WHISPER IS IF SOMEONE WERE HIDING IN IT, THE SAME WAY SOMEONE MUST HAVE HIDDEN IN THE BASE OF THE DOLLHOUSE.
THE LOCKET WE FOUND PROVED THAT. I ONLY HOPED CHIEF McGINNIS WOULD GET A COURT ORDER NOW TO OPEN THE BASE!

IN ANY CASE, NOW THAT I WAS ONTO SOMETHING, I COULDN'T LET THIS MYSTERY GO, EVEN IF THE VICTIM COULD BE *ME!*
MAYBE WE SHOULD CHEAT A LITTLE ON *NOSTALGIA WEEK* AND DO SOME *INTERNET* RESEARCH ON HAUNTED DOLL-HOUSES BACK AT NANCY'S!
GET *REAL,* BESS. WE'RE NOT GOING BACK TO NANCY'S. GET A LOAD OF THAT *LOOK* ON HER FACE!
NO?
NOPE.
WE'RE GOING TO THAT *CREEPY* HOUSE ON LARKSPUR LANE, AREN'T WE?
YUP.
NOTHING LIKE A *GOOD* FRIEND. THEY KNOW YOU SO WELL, SOMETIMES YOU *BARELY* HAVE TO TALK!
N2701

ABOUT 80 YEARS AGO, LARKSPUR LANE, JUST OUTSIDE OF TOWN, WAS WHERE THE RICHEST RIVER HEIGHTS CITIZENS OWNED WEEKEND HOMES.
THESE DAYS, IT WAS BARELY A ROAD!
HM! THAT KNOCKING CAN'T BE GOOD! COULD BE YOUR OIL, OR THE BEARINGS, OR IT COULD MEAN YOU'RE JUST...
KLUNK
KLUNK
...OUT OF GAS.
Y'KNOW, NANCE, I'M NOT EVEN MAD! I THINK IT'S PRETTY AMAZING YOU KEPT THE TANK FULL THIS LONG!

SIGH.
ONLY BECAUSE HANNAH FILLED IT FOR ME, TWICE!
ANOTHER THING MY FRIENDS KNOW ABOUT ME IS SOMETIMES I GET SO WRAPPED-UP IN A CASE, I FORGET EVERYTHING ELSE!
AWW... I WAS JUST GETTING USED TO MY HYBRID, WHICH ONLY RAN OUT OF GAS EVERY OTHER WEEK!
OH, YOU DON'T HAVE TO BANG YOUR HEAD AGAINST THE STEERING WHEEL, SWEETIE!
LET HER, BESS. IT'LL SAVE ME THE TROUBLE.
AND OF COURSE WE DON'T HAVE OUR CELL PHONES! AFTER ALL, IT'S NOSTALGIA WEEK! WHOOP DEE DOO!
YOU REALLY HAVE TO WONDER HOW ANYONE SOLVED CRIMES BACK THEN!

I'D LIKE TO SAY THAT AT LEAST I REMEMBERED AN UMBRELLA, BUT HANNAH PACKED THAT, TOO!
I KNOW NOSTALGIA ISN'T YOUR THING, GEORGE, BUT HOW ABOUT CUTTING SOME SLACK FOR AN OLD FRIEND?
AW, DON'T LISTEN TO ME! I JUST MISS MY PC, MY PDA, MY LCD TV AND ALL THOSE OTHER BEAUTIFUL INITIALS.
PLUS, I'M COLD AND WE'RE WALKING TO A CREEPY HOUSE WHERE YOU MAY DIE.
BUT WHEREVER YOU GO NANCY, YOU KNOW I'LL BE THERE.
A CREEPY HOUSE WHERE I MAY DIE.
I KNEW GEORGE WAS SORT OF JOKING AROUND, BUT WHEN I SAW THE TOP OF THE MANSION STICK ITS HEAD ABOVE THE TREES, I FELT PRETTY SMALL AND SCARED.
AS IF I WERE A DOLL.

NOSTALGIA WEEK ASIDE, THE 1930s WERE NOT ALL FUN AND GAMES.
AFTER A HUGE STOCK MARKET CRASH IN 1929, MILLIONS OF PEOPLE WERE SUDDENLY POOR AND OUT OF WORK.
THAT'S WHY LARKSPUR LANE WAS DESERTED. IT WAS LIKE A GHOST OF WHAT WAS CALLED THE GREAT DEPRESSION.
LOOK! CHIEF McGINNIS HAS SOMEONE WATCHING THE PLACE! WE CAN GET A RIDE HOME!
NO! I'M GLAD HE'S THERE TOO, BUT FIRST I WANT TO TAKE A LOOK AROUND!
I'VE GOT A HUNCH THE SOLUTION TO THE MYSTERY IS IN THAT HOUSE, AND I'M NOT LEAVING YET!

OKAY, FINE! SO WE'LL GET A LITTLE MORE SOAKED. BUT HOW DO WE GET IN? THAT PLACE IS LOCKED UP!
MY DAD HAD A CLIENT WHO BOUGHT THE HOUSE LAST SUMMER, SO WE CAME OUT TO VISIT.
I HAPPEN TO KNOW A SET OF KEYS ARE HIDDEN...
INSIDE THIS HOLLOW OAK!
IF YOU CAN REMEMBER THAT, WHY NOT GAS?
THAT'S EASY. GAS ISN'T DIRECTLY RELATED TO THE CASE!
SHH! LET'S GO AROUND BACK TO KEEP OUT OF SIGHT OF THE SQUAD CAR!

WOW! TALK ABOUT ABANDONED! THEY EVEN TOOK THE KITCHEN SINK!
AT LEAST IT'S RAINING LESS INSIDE HERE.
ARE WE USING BATTERIES FROM THE 1930s, TOO? THE OLD FLASHLIGHTS ARE GOING DIM FAST!
I GUESS WE'RE LUCKY THEY'RE WORKING AT ALL!
OH, NANCY, WE'RE NOT LUCKY AT ALL! I MEAN, SHOULD WE EVEN BE HERE? GHOSTS OR NOT, THAT DOLLHOUSE SHOWED YOU DEAD!

RELAX, GEORGE! THIS ISN'T EXACTLY THE SAME AS THE DOLLHOUSE! THERE'S A POLICE CAR OUT FRONT, NOT THE ROADSTER! SO THINGS ARE ALREADY DIFFERENT!
SEE?
OOPS.
I SEE. BUT DO YOU SEE WHAT I SEE?
THE POLICE CAR IS GONE AND THE ROADSTER IS THERE!
JUST LIKE THE DOLL-HOUSE!

WE ARE SO OUT OF HERE!
WE'LL WALK BACK TO TOWN IF WE HAVE TO!
YOU GUYS DO WHAT YOU HAVE TO, BUT I'M CHECKING THIS HOUSE OUT.
BRAVERY ISN'T ABOUT NOT BEING SCARED, IT'S ABOUT DOING THE RIGHT THING EVEN IF YOU ARE SCARED.
I WAS SCARED, ALL RIGHT. I JUST HOPED I WAS DOING THE RIGHT THING!
OKAY, SO LET'S FOLLOW HER!
FINE, BUT... UM-- GEORGE, ARE YOU BREATHING HEAVY FROM THE RAIN?
NO. WHY?

EEP!
I HEARD SOME SHUFFLING BEHIND ME, SO I FIGURED BESS AND GEORGE WERE COMING ALONG.
I KNEW THEY WOULDN'T DESERT ME!
BUT THEY COULD BE SLOW POKES SOMETIMES.
ONCE, I'D SOLVED A WHOLE MYSTERY IN THE TIME IT TOOK THEM TO GET OUT OF THE CAR!
OF COURSE, OTHER TIMES, THEY'VE SAVED MY NECK, SO I WAS ALWAYS GLAD TO KNOW THEY WERE THERE.
OW! GET YOUR HAND OUT OF MY FACE PLEASE!
THAT'S NOT MY HAND, IT'S YOURS!

IF I REMEMBERED CORRECTLY, MY FATHER'S CLIENT COULDN'T DECIDE WHETHER TO *RENOVATE* OR TEAR THE PLACE DOWN!

IF YOU ASK ME, I'D VOTE FOR *TEARING* THE PLACE DOWN. EVERY TIME I TOOK A STEP, IT FELT LIKE THE *FLOOR* WOULD FALL OUT FROM UNDER ME!

FOR A WHILE, I WAS THINKING THERE WAS SOMETHING *SPECIAL* ABOUT THE CRIMES, A PAINTING THAT WAS WORTHLESS, A *FAKE* PEARL NECKLACE, AN OLD HORSE...

THERE JUST DIDN'T SEEM TO BE *ANY* CONNECTION!

THEN I STARTED THINKING MAYBE THERE WASN'T ANY CONNECTION.

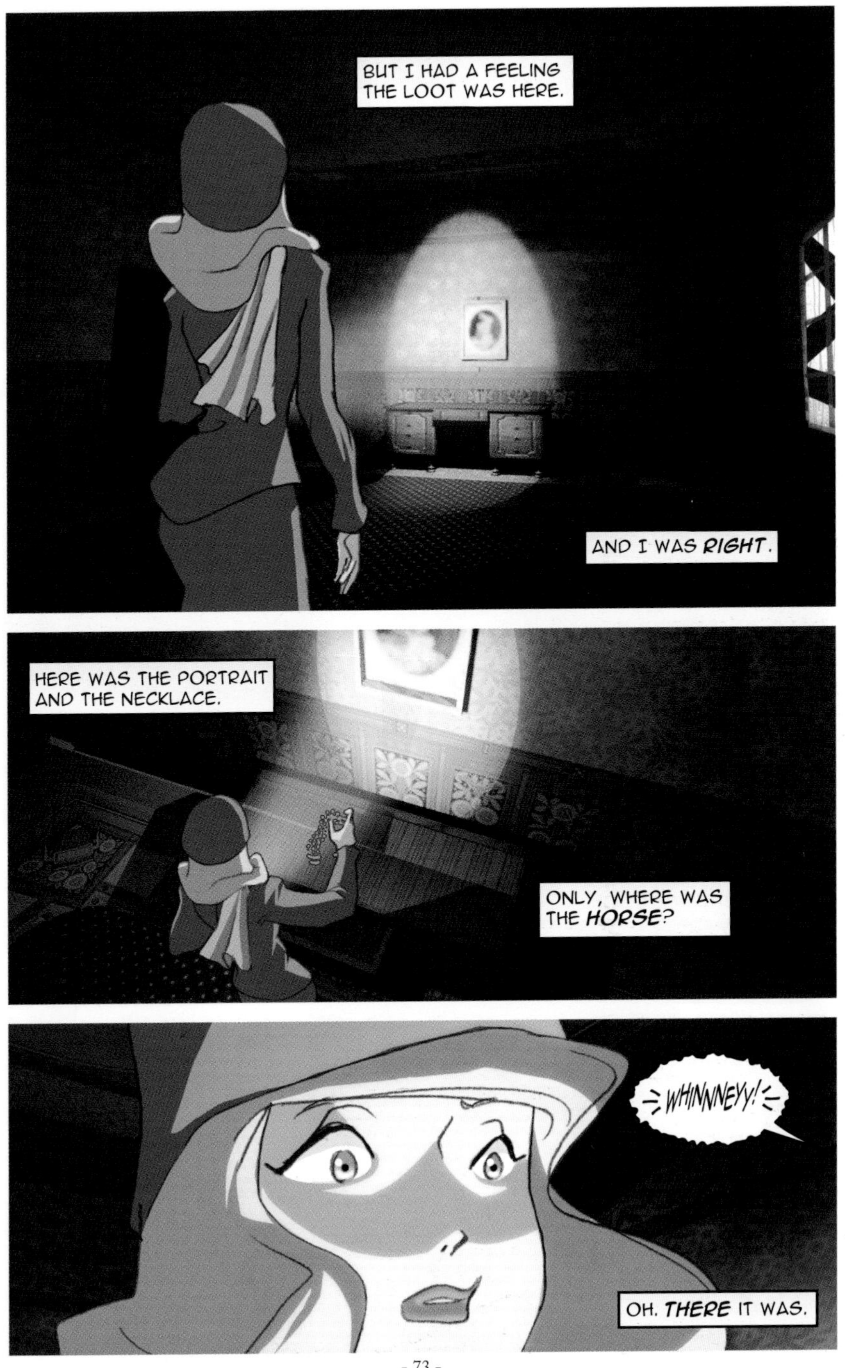
BUT I HAD A FEELING THE LOOT WAS HERE.
AND I WAS RIGHT.
HERE WAS THE PORTRAIT AND THE NECKLACE.
ONLY, WHERE WAS THE HORSE?
WHINNNEYY!
OH. THERE IT WAS.

-=WHINNNEYY!=-

BETWEEN THE RAIN AND THE SHADOWS, THE HORSE LOOKED LIKE IT WAS ***HAUNTING*** A ***BRIDGE*** THAT CROSSED THE STREAM OUT BACK.

HAUNTED ***DOLLHOUSE***, HAUNTED ***BRIDGE***, I WAS STARTING TO FEEL LIKE I WAS IN SOME OLD 1930s MYSTERY BOOK!

IN FACT, IT WAS LIKE SOME-ONE WAS SETTING IT UP TO ***BE*** A MYSTERY! LIKE THEY USED A DOLL THAT LOOKED LIKE ***ME*** BECAUSE THEY ***KNEW*** I'D COME LOOK!

BUT WHY? AND WHO?
IT SEEMED LIKE THE ANSWER SHOULD BE OBVIOUS, BUT LIKE I SAID, SOMETIMES I GET SO WRAPPED UP IN A MYSTERY, I DON'T SEE WHAT'S RIGHT IN FRONT OF ME.
OR BEHIND ME FOR THAT MATTER!

I HEARD THE DOOR LOCK. I GUESS WHOEVER SHOVED US DOWN HERE MEANS TO KEEP US!
AT LEAST WE'RE NOT ALONE!
IT'S THE POLICE OFFICER FROM THE SQUAD CAR!
IS HE ALIVE?
YES, HE'S JUST UNCON-SCIOUS!
OH, PLEASE, WAKE UP, MR. POLICE OFFICER! WE SURE COULD USE SOME HELP!

ANYTHING WE CAN USE FOR A PILLOW TO MAKE HIM COMFORT-ABLE? LOOK AROUND!
ANYTHING?
I'M ON IT!
NOTHING! JUST THIS OLD PHONE! AND IT'S DEAD AND USELESS, WHICH IS JUST HOW I FEEL!
BESS, REMEMBER HOW I SAID WHOEVER SHOVED US IN HERE LOCKED US IN?
YEAH?
WELL IT LOOKS LIKE HE LOCKED US IN WITH HIM! YIKES!

BESS! HELP!
WHAM
HEY, I GUESS THAT PHONE WASN'T SO USELESS AFTER ALL!

NOW WHY WOULD SOMEONE GO THROUGH ALL THE *TROUBLE* OF LURING ME TO A CREEPY HOUSE? SURE, I WAS PRETTY WELL KNOWN FOR BEING A *DETECTIVE*...

OH. THE PIECES JUST FELL TOGETHER. IT WAS LIKE A SECRET PANEL OPENING IN MY HEAD.

AND, BY THE WAY, AT ABOUT THE SAME TIME, A *REAL* SECRET PANEL OPENED UP IN THE ROOM.

BEYOND IT WAS A HIDDEN STAIRCASE, LEADING UP.

I WONDERED IF MY DAD'S CLIENT KNEW ABOUT ALL THE *EXTRA FEATURES* THE HOUSE HAD. MAYBE THERE WAS A *DUNGEON* SOMEWHERE, TOO.

ANYWAY, WHAT I FIGURED OUT WAS THAT SOMEONE MIGHT LEAD ME HERE *BECAUSE* I WAS KNOWN FOR BEING HOPELESSLY *CURIOUS* AND TRYING TO FIND THE *TRUTH*.

I'M ALSO PROUD TO SAY THAT I'M *TRUSTWORTHY*.

SO, IF SOMETHING HAPPENED TO ME, OR I STARTED TO BELIEVE IN THE HAUNTED DOLLHOUSE, LOTS OF OTHER PEOPLE WOULD, TOO.
SO THE QUESTION NOW WAS, WHO WOULD WANT EVERYONE TO BELIEVE IN A HAUNTED DOLLHOUSE?
WHOEVER IT WAS MADE SURE EVERYTHING HERE WOULD LOOK JUST LIKE THE SCENE BACK IN CITY HALL.THEY EVEN MADE SURE MY CAR WOULD BE HERE.
THERE WAS ONLY ONE THING MISSING.
THE PERSON WHO KILLS ME!

ALL OF A SUDDEN, I DIDN'T THINK CURIOSITY WAS SUCH A GREAT CHARACTER TRAIT!
IT IS, AFTER ALL, WHAT PUTS ME IN SITUATIONS LIKE THIS IN THE FIRST PLACE.
ON THE OTHER HAND, IT'S ALSO WHAT HELPS ME FIGURE THINGS OUT!
YOU'RE NO VISITOR FROM THE SPIRIT WORLD, THAT'S FOR SURE! IN FACT, I'M PRETTY SURE YOU'RE...

EMMA BLAVATSKY!
BUT WHY DO YOU WANT EVERYONE TO THINK YOUR DOLLHOUSE IS HAUNTED?
BECAUSE, YOU SILLY CHILD, I'M BROKE AND NEED MONEY! LOTS OF IT!
WHEN PEOPLE BELIEVE THE DOLLHOUSE IS HAUNTED, I'LL SELL IT FOR A FORTUNE, ALONG WITH THE BOOK AND MOVIE RIGHTS!
I SMUGGLED MY NEPHEW RAUL INTO THIS COUNTRY TO HELP. HE WAS HIDDEN IN THE BASE, REARRANGING THE DOLLS!
"THEN HE WOULD SNEAK OUT AND PERFORM THE CRIME!"
"I TOLD HIM NOT TO WEAR THAT STUPID BRACELET, BUT IT CONTAINED AN IVORY CHARM HIS MOTHER GAVE HIM, SO HE REFUSED TO LISTEN!"

SO YOU'RE CONFESS-ING?
WHY NOT? YOU WON'T BE AROUND TO TELL ANYONE!

UH-OH.

AHHHHHHHHHH!

HELP ME! HELP!
IT'S KIND OF SAD HOW PEOPLE WHO ARE TRYING TO KILL YOU ONE MINUTE, SOMETIMES BEG YOU FOR THEIR LIVES THE NEXT.
I'M SORRY! I CONFESS! I DON'T EVEN BELIEVE IN AN AFTERLIFE! IT WAS ALL A LIE! I JUST DON'T WANT TO DIE!
THANKS FOR THE CONFESSION, BUT I WOULD'VE SAVED YOU ANYWAY.
SOME OF US AREN'T KILLERS, YOU KNOW.

I JUST WANTED MY GOLDEN YEARS TO BE COMFORTABLE! I CAN'T BELIEVE I WAS ACTUALLY WILLING TO KILL FOR THAT!
I PUT SOME GAS IN YOUR CAR TO BRING IT HERE. WE'LL USE IT TO GO TO THE POLICE.
NO MORE TROUBLE FROM ME, I SWEAR!
REMEMBER HOW I SAID I WAS TRUSTWORTHY?
NO MORE TROUBLE FROM ME ONCE YOU'RE DEAD THAT IS, YOU LITTLE FOOL! HA!
WELL, SOME PEOPLE JUST AREN'T!
RAUL, THERE YOU ARE! HELP ME WITH THE GIRL!
WE CAN CARRY HER BACK UP AND THROW HER OFF THE ROOF! THE PLAN WILL STILL WORK!

I'M AFRAID HE'S NOT IN ANY POSITION TO DO THAT, MRS. BLAVATSKY.
BUT I **DO** THANK YOU FOR CONFESSING TO ATTEMPTED **MURDER**! IT WILL MAKE A NICE **ADDITION** TO THE CRIMINAL CHARGES THAT WILL BE FILED AGAINST YOU!

NO!
GOOD TO SEE YOU, CHIEF McGINNIS, AS ALWAYS!

BUT HOW DID YOU **KNOW** TO COME OUT HERE? RAUL KNOCKED OUT YOUR OFFICER RIGHT **AFTER** HE RADIOED TO TELL YOU EVERYTHING WAS **QUIET**!
AH, BUT I RECEIVED **ANOTHER** CALL!

TA-DA!
BEST FRIENDS TO THE RESCUE! WE KNOCKED OUT RAUL AND CALLED CHIEF McGINNIS!
AND WE DIDN'T EVEN HAVE TO BREAK FAITH WITH NOSTALGIA WEEK TO DO IT! BETWEEN MY MECHANICAL SMARTS AND GEORGE'S TECHNICAL SAVVY, WE REWIRED THIS OLD 1930s PHONE!
I GUESS THE NEW OWNER TURNED ON THE PHONE SERVICE, BECAUSE WHEN WE PLUGGED IT IN, IT WORKED!
MAYBE GEORGE AND I SHOULD OPEN OUR OWN DETECTIVE BUSINESS!
OR AT LEAST A REPAIR SHOP! BUT THANKS, GUYS!

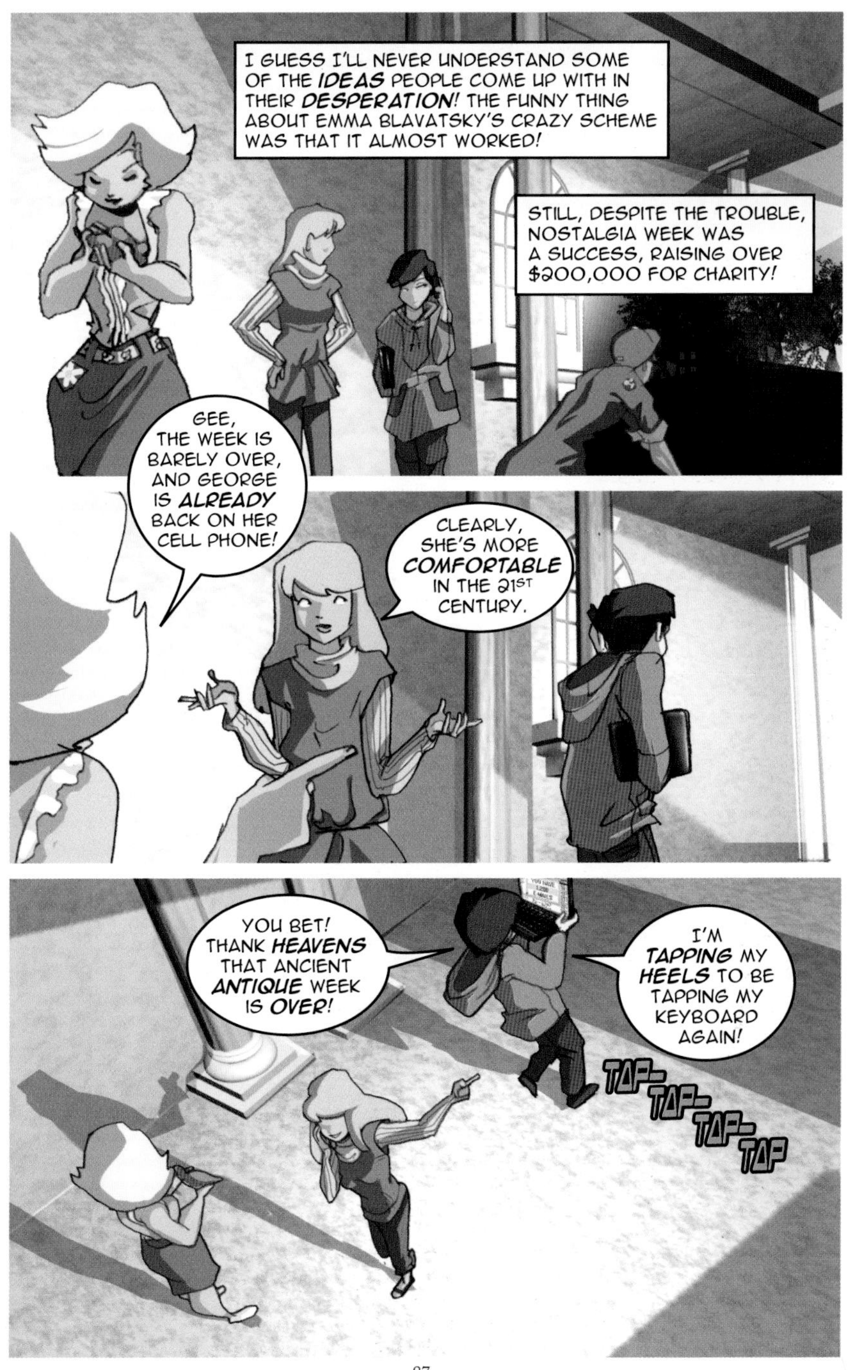

I GUESS I'LL NEVER UNDERSTAND SOME OF THE IDEAS PEOPLE COME UP WITH IN THEIR DESPERATION! THE FUNNY THING ABOUT EMMA BLAVATSKY'S CRAZY SCHEME WAS THAT IT ALMOST WORKED!
STILL, DESPITE THE TROUBLE, NOSTALGIA WEEK WAS A SUCCESS, RAISING OVER $200,000 FOR CHARITY!
GEE, THE WEEK IS BARELY OVER, AND GEORGE IS ALREADY BACK ON HER CELL PHONE!
CLEARLY, SHE'S MORE COMFORTABLE IN THE 21ST CENTURY.
YOU BET! THANK HEAVENS THAT ANCIENT ANTIQUE WEEK IS OVER!
I'M TAPPING MY HEELS TO BE TAPPING MY KEYBOARD AGAIN!
TAP- TAP- TAP- TAP

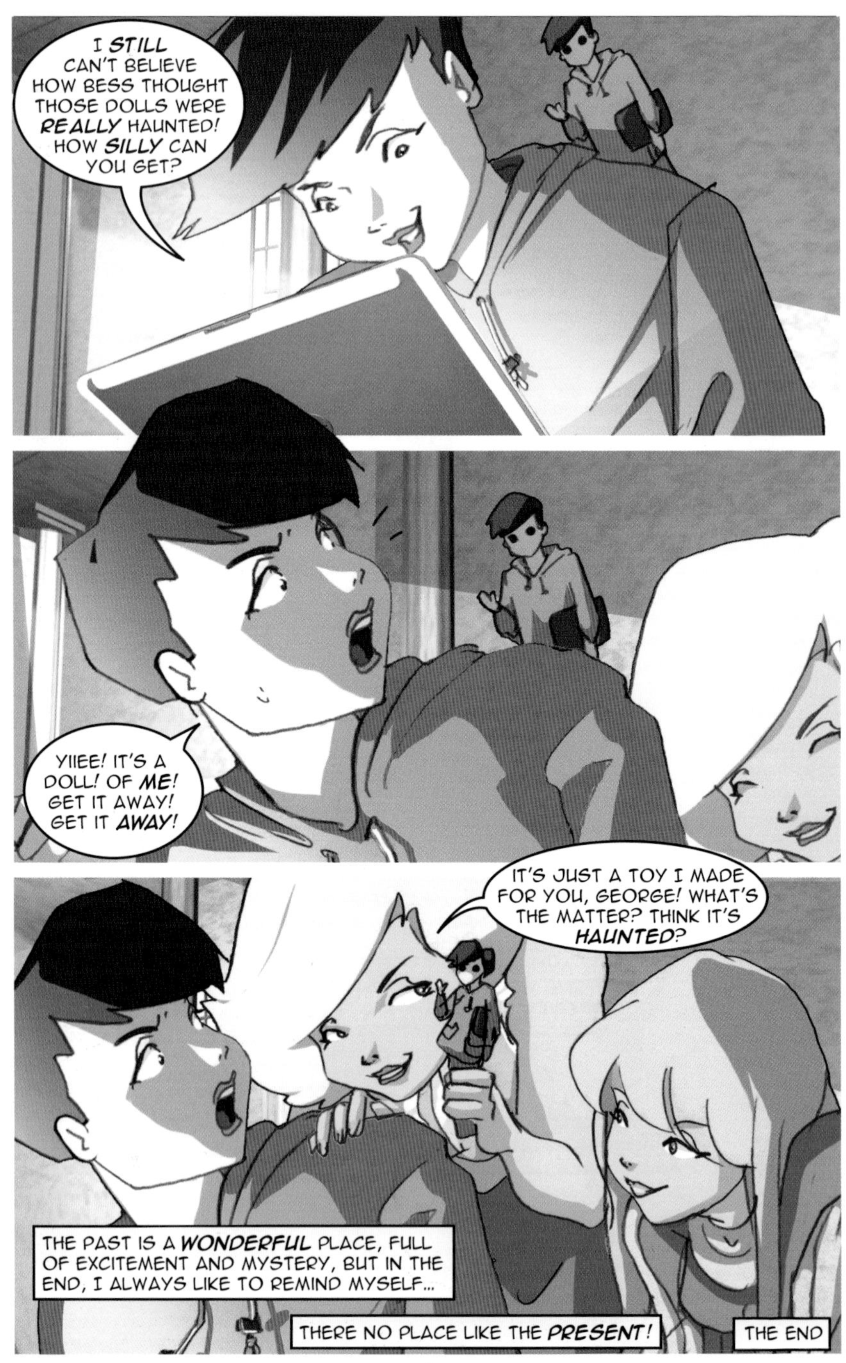
I STILL CAN'T BELIEVE HOW BESS THOUGHT THOSE DOLLS WERE REALLY HAUNTED! HOW SILLY CAN YOU GET?
YIIEE! IT'S A DOLL! OF ME! GET IT AWAY! GET IT AWAY!
IT'S JUST A TOY I MADE FOR YOU, GEORGE! WHAT'S THE MATTER? THINK IT'S HAUNTED?
THE PAST IS A WONDERFUL PLACE, FULL OF EXCITEMENT AND MYSTERY, BUT IN THE END, I ALWAYS LIKE TO REMIND MYSELF...
THERE NO PLACE LIKE THE PRESENT!
THE END

NANCY DREW HERE, DEALING WITH A DIFFERENT KIND OF MYSTERY -THE MYSTERY OF MODERN TECHNOLOGY!

I THINK COMPUTERS ARE TERRIFIC - EXCEPT WHEN THEY DON'T **WORK**.

GEORGE COULD CLEAR THIS UP IN A MINUTE, BUT SHE AND BESS WERE AT A FAMILY REUNION IN OHIO AND I DIDN'T WANT TO DRAG HER AWAY FROM THE PARTY.

AGHHH!

THE GIRL WHO WASN'T THERE

CHAPTER ONE: HERE, THERE AND EVERYWHERE!

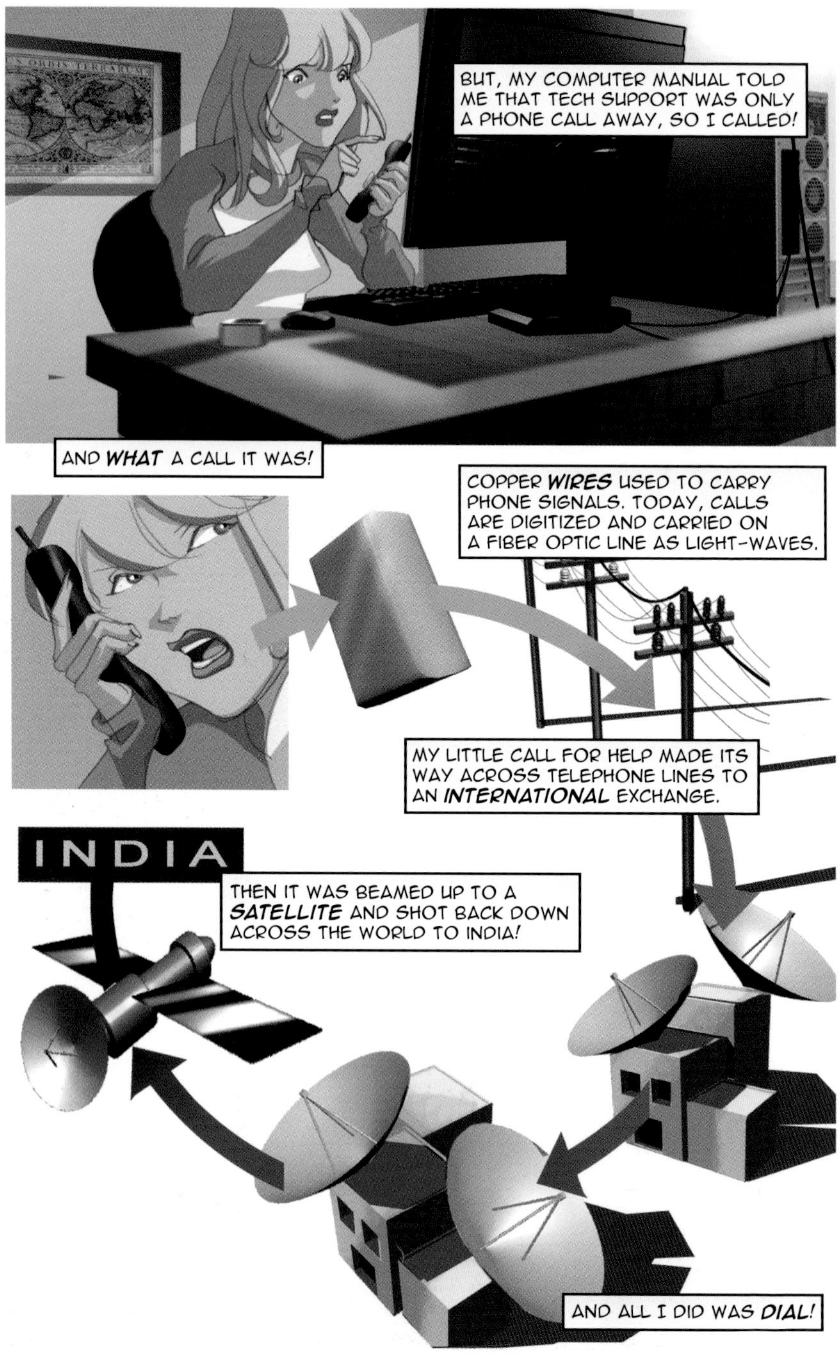
BUT, MY COMPUTER MANUAL TOLD ME THAT TECH SUPPORT WAS ONLY A PHONE CALL AWAY, SO I CALLED!
AND *WHAT* A CALL IT WAS!
COPPER *WIRES* USED TO CARRY PHONE SIGNALS. TODAY, CALLS ARE DIGITIZED AND CARRIED ON A FIBER OPTIC LINE AS LIGHT-WAVES.
MY LITTLE CALL FOR HELP MADE ITS WAY ACROSS TELEPHONE LINES TO AN *INTERNATIONAL* EXCHANGE.
INDIA
THEN IT WAS BEAMED UP TO A *SATELLITE* AND SHOT BACK DOWN ACROSS THE WORLD TO INDIA!
AND ALL I DID WAS *DIAL*!

NANCY DREW, YES, I HAVE YOUR RECORDS HERE. LOOKS LIKE YOU'RE DUE FOR AN OS UPDATE.
PLEASE HOLD ON WHILE I TAKE CARE OF THAT FOR YOU!
IT'S FIXED! HOW CAN I *THANK* YOU?
WELL, YOU COULD TELL ME IF YOU'RE NANCY DREW THE GIRL *DETECTIVE*, WHO I LIKE TO READ ABOUT ON THE WEB!
WOW, I HAD *NO* IDEA PEOPLE HAD HEARD OF ME, BUT I GUESS SOME OF MY CASES ARE PRETTY FAMOUS. WHERE ARE YOU LOCATED?
WELL, SINCE YOU ASKED, I CAN TELL YOU I'M IN NEW DELHI, INDIA!
YOU NEVER KNOW *WHEN* YOU'LL MAKE A NEW FRIEND, OR *WHERE*.

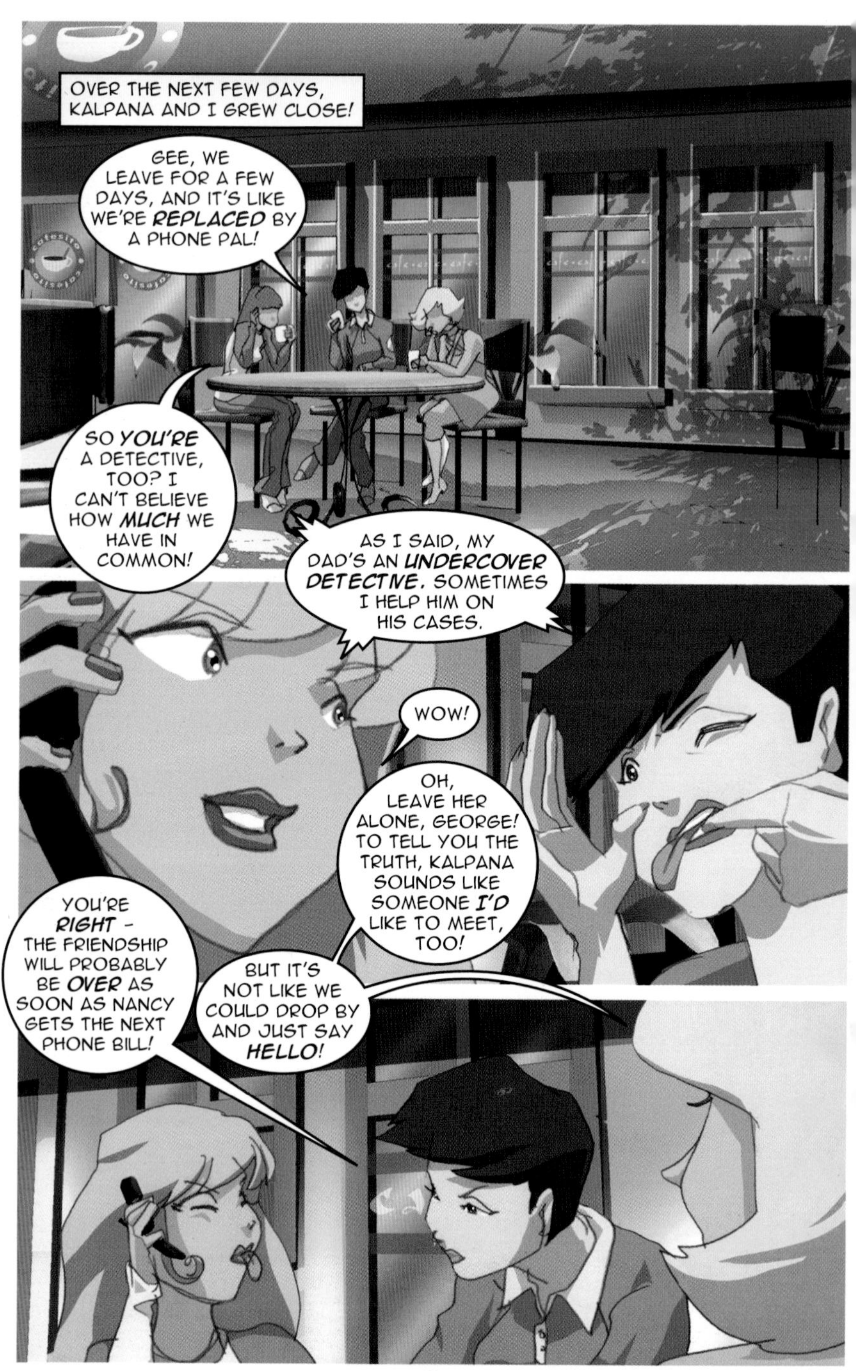
OVER THE NEXT FEW DAYS, KALPANA AND I GREW CLOSE!
GEE, WE LEAVE FOR A FEW DAYS, AND IT'S LIKE WE'RE REPLACED BY A PHONE PAL!
SO YOU'RE A DETECTIVE, TOO? I CAN'T BELIEVE HOW MUCH WE HAVE IN COMMON!
AS I SAID, MY DAD'S AN UNDERCOVER DETECTIVE. SOMETIMES I HELP HIM ON HIS CASES.
WOW!
OH, LEAVE HER ALONE, GEORGE! TO TELL YOU THE TRUTH, KALPANA SOUNDS LIKE SOMEONE I'D LIKE TO MEET, TOO!
YOU'RE RIGHT – THE FRIENDSHIP WILL PROBABLY BE OVER AS SOON AS NANCY GETS THE NEXT PHONE BILL!
BUT IT'S NOT LIKE WE COULD DROP BY AND JUST SAY HELLO!

THINGS ***DID*** SLOW DOWN WHEN THAT PHONE BILL ARRIVED, BUT WE STILL ***EMAILED*** EACH OTHER A LOT.

UNTIL ONE NIGHT, AT ***3:00 IN THE MORNING,*** MY CELL RANG.

BRPPPP
BRPPPPP

HELLO?
NANCY, IT'S KALPANA! THERE ARE MEN IN MY HOUSE, I THINK THEY WANT TO KIDNAP ME!
I DIDN'T KNOW WHO ELSE TO CALL! SOME OF THE POLICE HAVE BEEN BRIBED I...
AIEEEEEE!
HELLO? HELLO?
KALPANA?!

AFTER MY CALLS TO THE NEW DELHI POLICE GOT ME NOWHERE, I KNEW I SOMEHOW HAD TO GO HELP KALPANA ***MYSELF***.

FORTUNATELY, MY FATHER HAD BEEN PLANNING TO VISIT INDIA, TO MEET A CLIENT WHO PRODUCES FILMS.

FIGURING I'D NEED ALL THE HELP I COULD GET, I GOT HIM TO SPRING FOR TICKETS FOR BESS AND GEORGE, THOUGH I FOUND MYSELF WISHING THEY WOULD STAY IN ***THEIR*** SEATS, NOT ***MINE***.

BUT WHAT WOULD I DO WHEN WE GOT THERE?

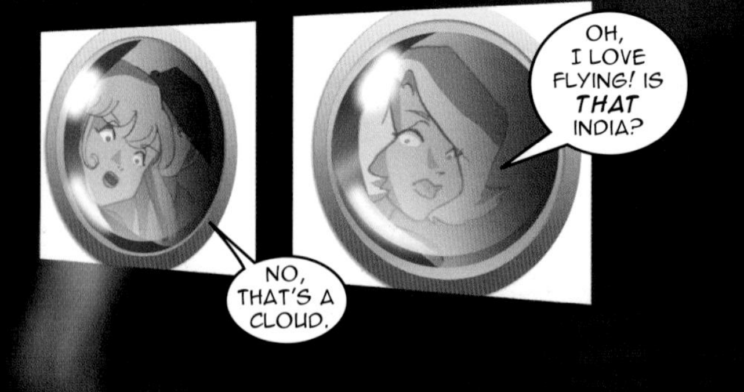

OH, I LOVE FLYING! IS THAT INDIA?
NO, THAT'S A CLOUD.

I DIDN'T EVEN KNOW KALPANA'S LAST NAME, OR WHAT SHE ***LOOKED*** LIKE!

GENERAL
INDIA IS THE LARGEST DEMOCRACY IN THE WORLD, HOME TO OVER ONE BILLION PEOPLE! AND IT FELT LIKE ALL OF THEM WERE IN THE CAPITAL, NEW DELHI!
AND IN A WAY, THEY WERE! NEW DELHI'S A CITY OF MIGRANTS, FULL OF PEOPLE FROM ALL OVER INDIA.
WOW! WHAT A FASCINATING PLACE! AND DIG THAT STRANGE, LOUD MUSIC!
leone del bambino
THAT'S MY LAPTOP! I'VE GOT IT PLAYING A HOT NEW TUNE!
MY FATHER WILL GET OUR BAGS TO THE HOTEL.
MEANWHILE, I'VE GOT THE ADDRESS OF THE CALL CENTER KALPANA SAID SHE WORKED AT.
SO HOP IN!
WHERE? THE FRONT SEAT'S MISSING!
IT'S AN AUTO-RICKSHAW, BESS. NANCY'S NOT THE ONLY ONE WHO DID SOME RESEARCH!
I ALSO READ THAT THEY GO PRETTY FAST. SO...

...HOLD ON TIGHT!
OUR DRIVER TOOK US ON THE SCENIC ROUTE, THROUGH VIJAY CHOWK, THE VICTORY SQUARE, WHERE THE MAIN GOVERNMENT BUILDINGS ARE.
SOME OF THE ARCHITECTURE HERE HAD A BRITISH INFLUENCE, FROM THE DAYS WHEN INDIA WAS A COLONY OF ENGLAND.
INDIA CELEBRATED ITS FIRST INDEPENDENCE DAY IN 1947, THANKS TO WHAT MAY HAVE BEEN THE WORLD'S FIRST PEACEFUL REVOLUTION, LED BY MOHATMA GHANDI.
AHHHH!

OUR DESTINATION WAS GURGUAN, JUST OUTSIDE DELHI. NEARLY HALF OF INDIA'S CALL CENTERS ARE HERE. THE PLACE LOOKED PRETTY MUCH LIKE A CORPORATE HQ BACK HOME.
I WAS WORRIED ABOUT SPEAKING *HINDI*, THE NATIONAL LANGUAGE, BUT IT TURNED OUT MANY PEOPLE SPEAK *ENGLISH* AS WELL.
A MISSING EMPLOYEE NAMED KALPANA? I DON'T KNOW HER MYSELF, BUT LET ME CHECK THE COMPUTER...
SORRY, THERE IS *NO ONE* NAMED KALPANA WORKING HERE.
WHAT? THAT'S NOT *POSSIBLE*!
WE INSTRUCT OUR WORKERS NOT TO USE THEIR *REAL* NAMES. CUSTOMERS FEEL MORE COMFORTABLE WITH AMERICAN NAMES.
THOUGH KALPANA IS HARDLY AMERICAN, IS IT? YOU CAN ASK AROUND FOR HER IF YOU LIKE.

WE TALKED TO EVERYONE, AND NOBODY'S HEARD OF HER!
I WISH SHE'D SENT ME A PHOTO!
OH, A MONKEY! THEY'RE LIKE SQUIRRELS AROUND HERE!
EXCUSE ME, MISS! PLEASE DO NOT FEED THE RHESUS MACAQUE! IF THEY THINK THERE'S FOOD HERE, THEY'LL MOVE INTO THE BUILDING!
MOVE IN?
OH, YES! THE MONKEYS ARE RESPECTED BY HINDUS AS MANIFES-TATIONS OF THE MONKEY GOD, HANUMAN, SO MANY PEOPLE FEED THEM.
"THEY EVEN OVERRAN SOME OF OUR GOVERNMENT BUILDINGS! THE MONKEYS BROKE AND STOLE THINGS, TERRORIZING THE EMPLOYEES!"
"THEY TRIED USING HIGH FREQUENCY SOUNDS TO DRIVE THEM OUT, BUT IT DIDN'T WORK!"

OKAY.
HARD TO BELIEVE THIS CUTE FELLOW WOULD HURT ANYONE.
EVEN SO, MAYBE YOU SHOULD STEP BACK A LITTLE, BESS.
OW!
EEEEP!
YIKES! GUESS HE HAS SIMILAR TASTE IN ACCESSORIES, HUH? NO BLOOD, THOUGH, HE JUST NIPPED YOU.
WELL, SINCE HE DIDN'T WANT MY SANDWICH, NOW AT LEAST HE CAN BUY HIS OWN.

THANKS FOR TRYING TO WARN US. MY NAME IS NANCY DREW, AND THESE ARE MY FRIENDS BESS AND GEORGE.
GOOD TO MEET YOU. MY NAME IS DARSHAN.
DARSHAN! YOU DELIVER HOT LUNCHES TO THE WORKERS! KALPANA TOLD ME ALL ABOUT YOU! CUTE, DARK HAIR, ABOUT 5'7", AND A LITTLE SCAR OVER YOUR CHEEK!
YOU MUST HAVE ME CONFUSED WITH SOMEONE ELSE!
I'M SORRY, BUT I DEFINITELY DON'T KNOW ANYONE NAMED KALPANA!

AND IF YOU'RE SMART, YOU DON'T KNOW HER EITHER!
I'M SORRY, I MUST GO.
Leone del bambino
SO, THAT COUNTS AS A CLUE, RIGHT?
YUP.
AND WE'LL FOLLOW HIM AFTER HE STOPS WORK, RIGHT?
YUP.
THERE HE IS. LET'S GO.
GREAT! I WAS GETTING TIRED OF CHECKING THE TREES FOR MORE MONKEYS!

SINCE WE SORT OF STUCK OUT AS LIGHT-SKINNED FOREIGNERS, IT WASN'T EASY STAYING UNSEEN!
BUT THANKS TO THE CROWDS AND THE SETTING SUN, WE MANAGED.
WE FOLLOWED DARSHAN TO ONE OF THE POOR SHANTY TOWNS THAT SURROUND THE CITY.
IT'S VERY DIFFICULT AND EXPENSIVE TO FIND A PLACE TO LIVE IN INDIA, AND THE COUNTRY HAS MANY HOMELESS.
IT WASN'T LONG BEFORE HE HAD VISITORS.
DARSHAN! GET OUT HERE! MOVE YOUR LAZY BUTT!

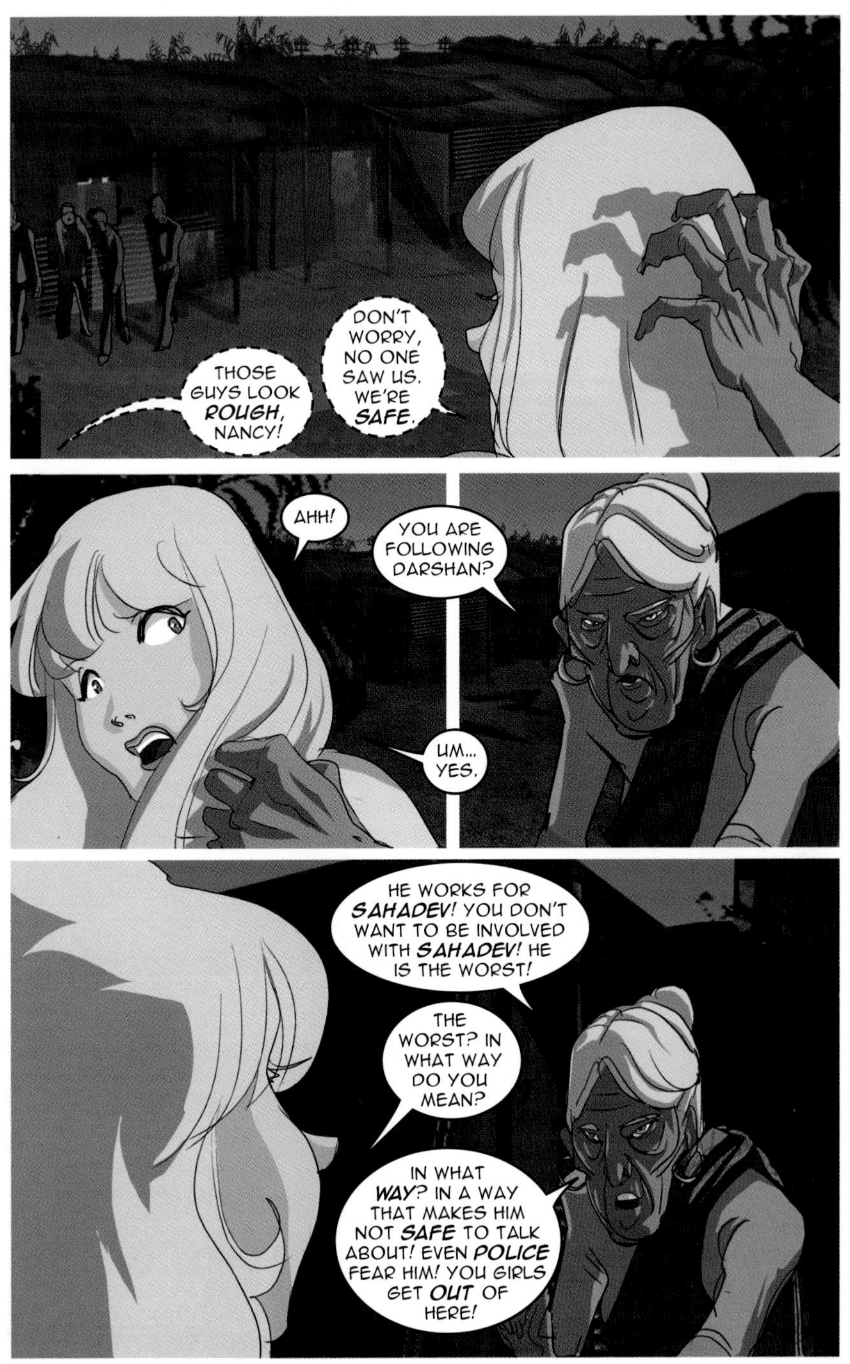
THOSE GUYS LOOK ROUGH, NANCY!
DON'T WORRY, NO ONE SAW US. WE'RE SAFE.
AHH!
YOU ARE FOLLOWING DARSHAN?
UM... YES.
HE WORKS FOR SAHADEV! YOU DON'T WANT TO BE INVOLVED WITH SAHADEV! HE IS THE WORST!
THE WORST? IN WHAT WAY DO YOU MEAN?
IN WHAT WAY? IN A WAY THAT MAKES HIM NOT SAFE TO TALK ABOUT! EVEN POLICE FEAR HIM! YOU GIRLS GET OUT OF HERE!

MAYBE SHE'S RIGHT.
OKAY, I'LL TRY THE POLICE AGAIN. BUT FIRST...
I WANT A LOOK INSIDE.
NANCY!
IT DIDN'T LOOK ANY BETTER ON THE INSIDE. I GUESSED THAT SAHADEV AND DARSHAN WERE INVOLVED IN SOME KIND OF CROOKED ACTIVITY.
AND WHILE I COULD SEE WHERE LIVING LIKE THIS MIGHT MAKE SOME-ONE TURN TO A LIFE OF CRIME...
...THAT DIDN'T MAKE IT RIGHT.
DARSHAN DIDN'T OWN VERY MUCH, SO I KNEW THAT PICTURE MUST BE VERY IMPORTANT TO HIM.
THEN I REALIZED WHO IT WAS.

ANY LUCK?
YES! I FOUND HER! OR AT LEAST HER *PICTURE*!
HOW DO YOU KNOW IT'S KALPANA?
BECAUSE IT'S GOT HER NAME AND ADDRESS ON THE BACK! SEE?
Kalpana Kaur
15 Parliament Street
New Delhi, Delhi
110001
WHICH MEANT WE HAD ONE *MORE* PLACE TO VISIT, KALPANA'S *HOME*!

I WAS HALF-HOPING KALPANA WOULD BE THERE, THAT THE WHOLE THING WAS SOME SORT OF MISTAKE, THAT MY FRIEND WAS PERFECTLY SAFE.
NO SUCH LUCK. THE HOUSE WAS TOTALLY ABANDONED.
HOW ABOUT THOSE POLICE NOW?
NOT YET!
YOU HEARD WHAT THAT WOMAN SAID, THE POLICE ARE AFRAID OF THIS SAHADEV.
I'VE A HUNCH HE'S BEHIND WHAT HAPPENED TO KALPANA, AND IF HE IS, I NEED MORE EVIDENCE FOR THE POLICE.
THE PHOTO ALONE DOESN'T TELL US WHAT HAPPENED. FOR STARTERS, I NEED TO FIND PROOF SHE LIVED HERE!

SO DID KALPANA EVER DESCRIBE HER HOUSE?
YES. HER ROOM WAS TOWARD THE BACK.
THIS WAY.
THERE'S NO ELECTRICITY, AND I CAN BARELY SEE MY OWN HAND, NANCY!
DID YOU BRING YOUR FLASH-LIGHT?
AS A DETECTIVE, YOU LEARN TO KEEP CERTAIN IMPORTANT TOOLS AROUND AT ALL TIMES.
RIGHT HERE.
A FLASHLIGHT IS PROBABLY THE MOST IMPORTANT.
IT'S TERRIBLY USEFUL AGAINST THE DARK.

BUT I NEVER EVEN THOUGHT ABOUT CARRYING SOMETHING TO USE AGAINST RHESUS MONKEYS!
EEP.

GEORGE, HOW LOUD CAN YOUR LAPTOP SPEAKERS GO?
P-PRETTY LOUD. I CUSTOMIZED THEM MYSELF. WHY?
I WAS JUST THINKING ABOUT WHAT DARSHAN SAID ABOUT HIGH FREQUENCY SOUNDS AND MONKEYS.
DIDN'T HE SAY IT DIDN'T WORK?!
YES, BUT I WAS HOPING...
...THEY JUST USED THE WRONG NOISE!

WHEW!
A NIP FROM ONE OF THOSE THINGS WAS BAD ENOUGH, BUT...
YOU SEE SOMETHING NANCY?
MAYBE.
KALPANA COMPLAINED HER ROOM HADN'T BEEN CHANGED SINCE SHE WAS A LITTLE GIRL.
THE WALLPAPER MADE HER FEEL LIKE HER DAD STILL THOUGHT OF HER AS A CHILD.
THIS PRETTY BALLOON PATTERN FITS THAT DESCRIPTION!
WHAT ELSE DID SHE TELL YOU, NANCY? HOW TO USE LAPTOP COMPUTERS AGAINST RHESUS MONKEYS?

NO.
WE JUST GOT LUCKY WITH THAT. BUT SHE *DID* TELL ME WHERE SHE KEPT HER *DIARY*.
I GUESS WITH ME HALFWAY AROUND THE *WORLD*, SHE WASN'T WORRIED I'D TRY TO *READ* IT!
AND NOW WE HAVE A REALLY *BIG* CLUE!
MAYBE IT'LL EVEN TELL US WHERE SHE WENT! HOORAY!
UH-OH. *NOT* HURRAY. WHAT'S WRONG, NANCE?
IT'S WRITTEN IN HINDI.

WELL, AT LEAST NOW WE KNOW SHE EXISTED!
EASY, BESS. IT'S NOT LIKE WE THOUGHT NANCY WAS TALKING TO HERSELF ON THE PHONE ALL THAT TIME.
I'M JUST REALLY WORRIED SOMETHING TERRIBLE MAY HAVE HAPPENED TO HER!
WE'VE GOT TO HAVE THIS DIARY TRANSLATED AS SOON AS POSSIBLE!
I'D LOVE TO GIVE YOU A RIDE, LADIES, BUT MY POOR VEHICLE HAS COLLAPSED!
MISTER, YOU BROKE DOWN IN JUST THE RIGHT PLACE!
HOW ABOUT IF I FIX YOUR AUTO-WHATEVER THING, YOU GIVE US A FREE LIFT TO OUR HOTEL?

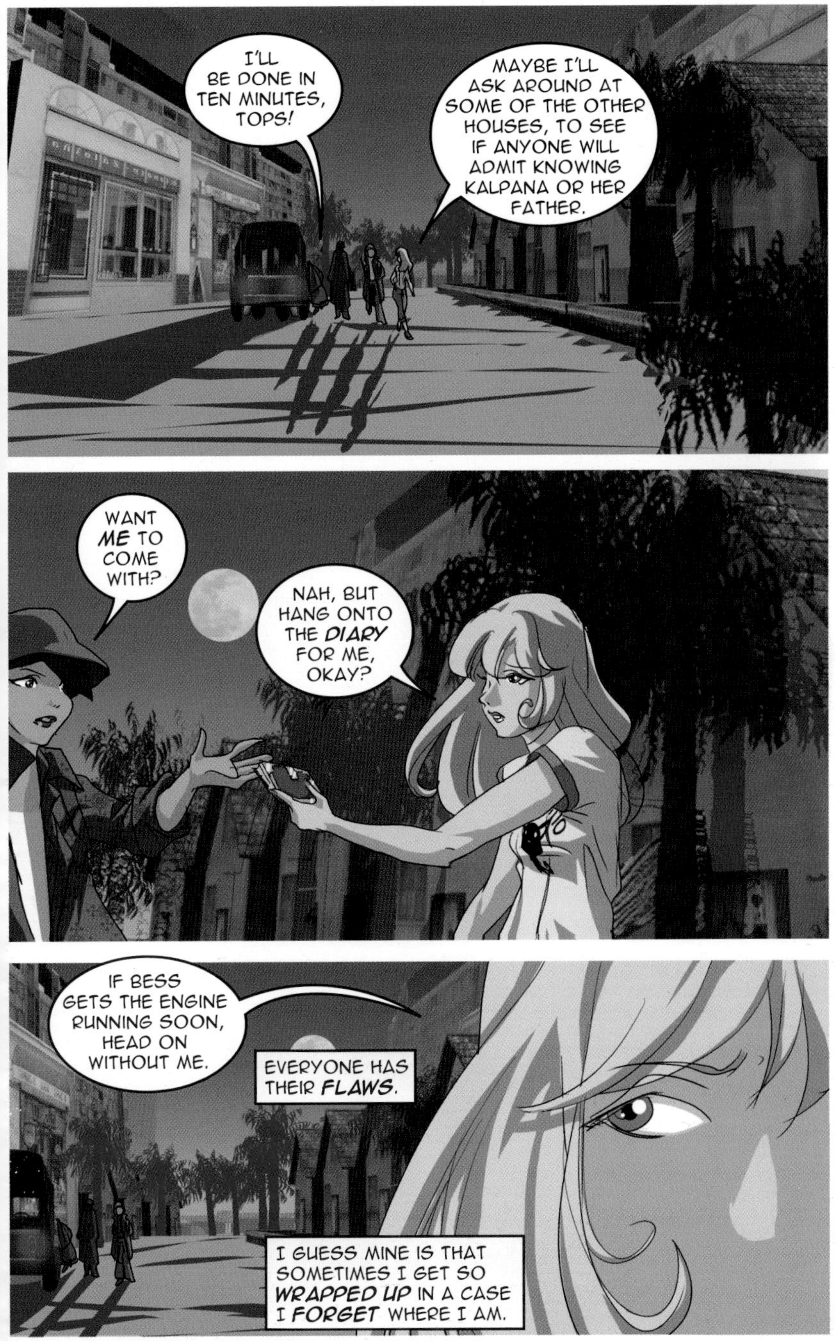
I'LL BE DONE IN TEN MINUTES, TOPS!
MAYBE I'LL ASK AROUND AT SOME OF THE OTHER HOUSES, TO SEE IF ANYONE WILL ADMIT KNOWING KALPANA OR HER FATHER.
WANT ME TO COME WITH?
NAH, BUT HANG ONTO THE DIARY FOR ME, OKAY?
IF BESS GETS THE ENGINE RUNNING SOON, HEAD ON WITHOUT ME.
EVERYONE HAS THEIR FLAWS.
I GUESS MINE IS THAT SOMETIMES I GET SO WRAPPED UP IN A CASE I FORGET WHERE I AM.

LIKE, THE FACT THAT I'M IN A STRANGE NEIGHBORHOOD IN A FOREIGN COUNTRY.
LOOKING FOR SOMEONE WHO MAY HAVE BEEN KIDNAPPED.
AND HER KIDNAPPERS MIGHT NOT WANT ME TO FIND HER.
I TOLD YOU YOU'D BE BETTER OFF PRETENDING YOU DIDN'T KNOW HER.
GASP
I'M PRETTY FAST ON MY FEET, AND I USUALLY MANAGE TO GET AWAY. BACK HOME CHIEF McGINNIS SAYS I'M JUST LIKE A RABBIT IN A BRIAR PATCH.
THAT MAY BE TRUE, BUT I DIDN'T SEE ANY BRIAR PATCHES HERE. ONLY MORE TROUBLE.

SO I HAD TO *IMPROVISE*.
AGHHH!
I HEADED AS FAST AS I COULD INTO THE ALLEY, FIGURING THAT EVEN IF THESE GOONS KNEW THE AREA, THE *DARKNESS* WOULD MAKE US MORE *EVEN*.

FOR AS LONG AS I COULD, I JUST *RAN*, FLAT OUT.
I WAS *SURE* I'D LOST THEM. AFTER ALL, I WAS PRETTY *LOST* MYSELF.

I ONLY HOPED I WAS CLOSE ENOUGH TO WHERE I *STARTED* TO FIND BESS AND GEORGE.
IF THEY HADN'T LEFT *WITHOUT* ME.

FORTUNATELY, I HAD MY HAND FLASHLIGHT.
OR MAYBE I SHOULD HAVE MADE THAT UN-FORTUNATELY.
IT MADE ME SORT OF MISS THE MONKEYS.
END CHAPTER ONE

NANCE! COME ON, GIRL! BESS, THE MAGIC MECHANIC, HAS OUR RIDE UP AND RUNNING!
I CAN'T SEE ANYTHING DOWN THERE! BUT I'M SURE SHE'S FINE! NANCY DREW CAN TAKE CARE OF HERSELF!
CHAPTER TWO: NANCY MAKES A SACRIFICE
HELP!

I THINK WHAT YOU MEAN IS WE'D BETTER TAKE CARE OF NANCY DREW!
YES, THAT'S WHAT I MEANT.
SIR, YOU SAID YOU OWED ME A FAVOR FOR FIXING YOUR AUTO-RICKSHAW-THINGY, RIGHT?
WELL, I'D LIKE TO BORROW IT!
CAN YOU EVEN DRIVE IT, MISS?
WE'RE GOING TO FIND OUT!

FASTER! FASTER!
HEY, BESS, NO ONE LIKES A BACKSEAT DRIVER!
BESIDES, I'M GAINING ON THEM!
HEY, THAT'S NOT EVEN A STREET!
SHEESH, BESS, THEY'RE KIDNAPPING! I DON'T THINK A LITTLE TRAFFIC VIOLATION IS GOING TO SLOW THEM DOWN!

SO IT'S NOT GOING TO SLOW *ME* DOWN, EITHER!
THRASH

"LOOK! THERE'S NANCY! I CAN SEE HER IN THE VAN!"

"HANG ON, BESS! I'M GOING TO TRY TO STEER THIS THING THROUGH THE *FENCE*!"

CRUNK
YIKES!
EEEP!

SKRULNNNNNNNNK
HISSSSSSSSSSSSSSSSS

YOUR FRIENDS ARE DEAD!
NO ONE WILL HELP YOU NOW!

NO! NO, THEY'RE NOT! THEY CAN'T BE!
HOLD HER.

PERHAPS YOU'RE RIGHT. PERHAPS THEY'RE NOT.
BUT YOU WILL BE SOON!

FOR A MINUTE, I THOUGHT I WAS BACK HOME IN RIVER HEIGHTS, LYING IN MY BED, HALF-ASLEEP.
I WONDERED IF MAYBE THE WHOLE PHONE CALL FROM KALPANA WAS JUST A *DREAM!*
BUT WHEN I REACHED OUT TO PULL MY NICE *WARM* BLANKET UP AROUND ME, ALL I FELT WAS *STRAW.*
SO, IT WASN'T A DREAM.
IT WAS A *NIGHTMARE!*

AWAKE? GOOD.
I AM SAHADEV, AND I WOULD LIKE VERY MUCH TO KNOW WHY YOU HAVE BEEN POKING AROUND MY BUSINESS!
IN A SITUATION LIKE THIS, I SAW NO POINT IN LYING!
I'M LOOKING FOR MY FRIEND, KALPANA! I MET HER ON THE PHONE, BACK IN THE UNITED STATES! SHE CALLED ME AND SAID SHE WAS IN DANGER!
I JUST WANT TO KNOW WHAT HAPPENED TO HER!
UNFORTUNATELY, SOMETIMES WHEN YOU'RE DEALING WITH CRIMINAL-TYPES, EVEN THE TRUTH WON'T HELP!
ALL THE WAY FROM THE UNITED STATES JUST TO FIND A PHONE PAL?
I DO NOT BELIEVE YOU!
SO I'LL ASK AGAIN, WHY ARE YOU HERE?
AND THIS TIME YOU'D BETTER TELL ME EVERY-THING!

OW.
OW. OW. OW.
OW.
NEXT TIME I DRIVE, OKAY?
YOU GOT IT.

THEY TOOK NANCY AND THEY GOT AWAY! WHAT DO WE DO?
FIRST, WE CALL THE POLICE AND HER DAD!

PERFECT. THE CELL'S NOT WORKING!
THIS IS AWFUL!
WE'RE ALL ALONE IN A STRANGE COUNTRY AND NANCY'S BEEN KID-NAPPED.
UH... BESS?
WE'RE NOT SO ALONE, REALLY.

EVENTUALLY SAHADEV LEFT ME ALONE TO THINK ABOUT TELLING HIM 'THE TRUTH.'
BUT ALL I **COULD** THINK ABOUT WAS A WAY TO GET OUT OF MY CELL AND TRYING TO FIND **KALPANA**!

HE WAS OBVIOUSLY PROTECTING A CRIMINAL RACKET, AND I HAD A HUNCH IT WAS SOMETHING **BIG**, MAYBE LIKE **SMUGGLING**!
OTHERWISE, HOW COULD HE AFFORD TO KEEP A **DUNGEON**?

THE LOCK LOOKED PRETTY **SIMPLE**, BUT IT TOOK ME A WHILE TO FIND A THICK ENOUGH STALK IN MY STRAW BED TO TRY **PICKING** IT WITH!

I DON'T KNOW A LOT ABOUT PICKING LOCKS, BUT I HAVE LEARNED A THING OR TWO!
I CAN OPEN MAYBE TWO OUT OF FIVE SINGLE CYLINDER LOCKS! I WAS HOPING THIS ONE WAS ONE OF THE TWO!
IT TURNED OUT, IT DIDN'T HAVE TO BE!
IT WAS ALREADY UNLOCKED!
HAD SOMEONE LEFT IT OPEN BY ACCIDENT?
MAYBE! RIGHT THEN AND THERE I DIDN'T WANT TO QUESTION MY LUCK!

IT WAS COOL AND DAMP, SO I KNEW I WAS PROBABLY UNDERGROUND.
THERE WERE A WHOLE BUNCH OF OTHER CELLS, SO MAYBE IT WAS AN OLD, ABANDONED PRISON! OR THE BASEMENT OF SOME OTHER TYPE OF STONE BUILDING.
THEN I HEARD SOMEONE CALLING!
IS SOMEONE THERE? PLEASE, I'M THIRSTY!
IT WAS A VOICE I RECOGNIZED IN A SECOND!
KALPANA!
NANCY DREW?

OH, NANCY! I CAN'T *BELIEVE* YOU CAME TO HELP ME!
CALM DOWN, KALPANA, WE'LL GET YOU OUT OF HERE! FIRST *TELL* ME, WHO IS SAHADEV AND WHY HAS HE KIDNAPPED US?
"HE'S A BIG *SMUGGLER* WITH TIES TO INTERNATIONAL ORGANIZED CRIME. HIS HANDS ARE *EVERYWHERE*, EVEN AT THE COMPANY WHERE I WORKED!"
"HE HAS PEOPLE TOO *TERRIFIED* TO SPEAK HIS NAME!"
THAT'S PROBABLY HOW THE COMPUTER RECORDS GOT WIPED *CLEAN,* AND WHY EVERYONE PRETENDED YOU DIDN'T *EXIST*!

"YOU KNOW MY FATHER IS A POLICE DETECTIVE, YES? HE'S WORKING UNDERCOVER IN SAHADEV'S ORGANIZATION, PRETENDING TO BE ONE OF HIS MEN!
"SAHADEV FOUND OUT ABOUT IT THROUGH HIS CORRUPT POLICE CONTACTS, BUT HE STILL DOESN'T KNOW WHO IN HIS ORGANIZATION IS MY FATHER! HIS DISGUISE IS PERFECT!
"SO, HE KIDNAPPED ME, HOPING MY FATHER WOULD GIVE HIMSELF UP, OR THAT I WOULD BETRAY HIM!
"BUT MY FATHER AND I KNOW THAT IF SAHADEV LEARNS WHO HE IS, OUR LIVES WILL BOTH BE FORFEIT!
I WASN'T EVEN SURE WHO I COULD TRUST AMONG THE POLICE OR MY OWN NEIGHBORS, SO I CALLED YOU, MY FRIEND!
AND YOU CAME! HOW CAN I THANK YOU?

THANK ME AFTER WE'RE SAFE!
UNGH! I WAS HOPING YOUR CELL WAS UNLOCKED, LIKE MINE, BUT NO SUCH LUCK!
MAYBE I CAN PICK THE LOCK.
WITH A PIECE OF HAY?
TRY USING THE BUCKLE OF MY BELT, INSTEAD!
A GIRL AFTER MY OWN HEART! GOOD THINKING!

GOT IT!
CLICK
THAT'S *WONDERFUL*! I WAS NEVER ANY GOOD AT LOCK PICKING MYSELF!
ME NEITHER! WE JUST GOT *LUCKY*!
LET'S SEE IF WE CAN STAY *LUCKY* ENOUGH TO GET OUT OF HERE!

THEY'RE BACK! WE HAVE TO HIDE!
HIDE? BUT WHERE?
TIME TO CHECK ON OUR TWO YOUNG CAPTIVES!
I STILL DON'T SEE WHY WE DON'T JUST KILL THEM! IF YOU'RE CONCERNED, I'LL DO IT MYSELF!

YOU'RE A GOOD MAN, VARIYA! LOYAL AND STRONG, BUT NOT QUITE SMART ENOUGH TO BE THE BOSS, EH?
I DO NOT KILL KALPANA BECAUSE SHE IS USEFUL!
THIS OTHER ONE, THIS NANCY DREW, SHE MAY NOT BE USEFUL MUCH LONGER.
IN WHICH CASE....
EH?
KALPANA IS GONE!

CHECK THE OTHER GIRL'S CELL, QUICKLY!

KALPANA, ARE YOU *FAST*?
RIGHT NOW I FEEL LIKE I COULD OUT-RACE A *MONGOOSE*!
THEN GET READY TO RUN....

NOW!

I HAVE TO ADMIT, WE WERE PRETTY FAST!
GET BACK HERE!
LITTLE FOOLS! I LEFT NANCY DREW'S CELL OPEN SO YOU WOULD FIND EACH OTHER!
ALL THE BETTER TO END YOUR HOPES OF ESCAPE!
UNFORTUNATELY, WE JUST WEREN'T FAST ENOUGH!

I'M TIRED OF THESE GAMES.
AND I THINK I KNOW A WAY TO GET WHAT I WANT.
I AM A WORSHIPPER OF KALI, DESTROYER OF WORLDS.
SHE HAS BROUGHT ME MUCH SUCCESS IN LIFE, PARTICULARLY IN DESTROYING MY ENEMIES.
AND KALI ALWAYS APPRECIATES A GOOD SACRIFICE!
GULP! SACRIFICE?
YES, IF KALPANA DOES NOT REVEAL HER FATHER'S IDENTITY, I WILL SACRIFICE YOU TO KALI!
YOU'RE BLUFFING!

AM I?
DON'T TELL HIM, KALPANA!
I CERTAINLY DIDN'T WANT HER TO **BETRAY** HER FATHER.
THEN AGAIN, I DIDN'T WANT TO BE **SACRIFICED**, EITHER! SO I TALKED **TOUGH**.
I'LL FIGURE A WAY OUT OF THIS!
I ONLY WISH I WAS AS **SURE** AS I WAS TRYING TO **SOUND**!

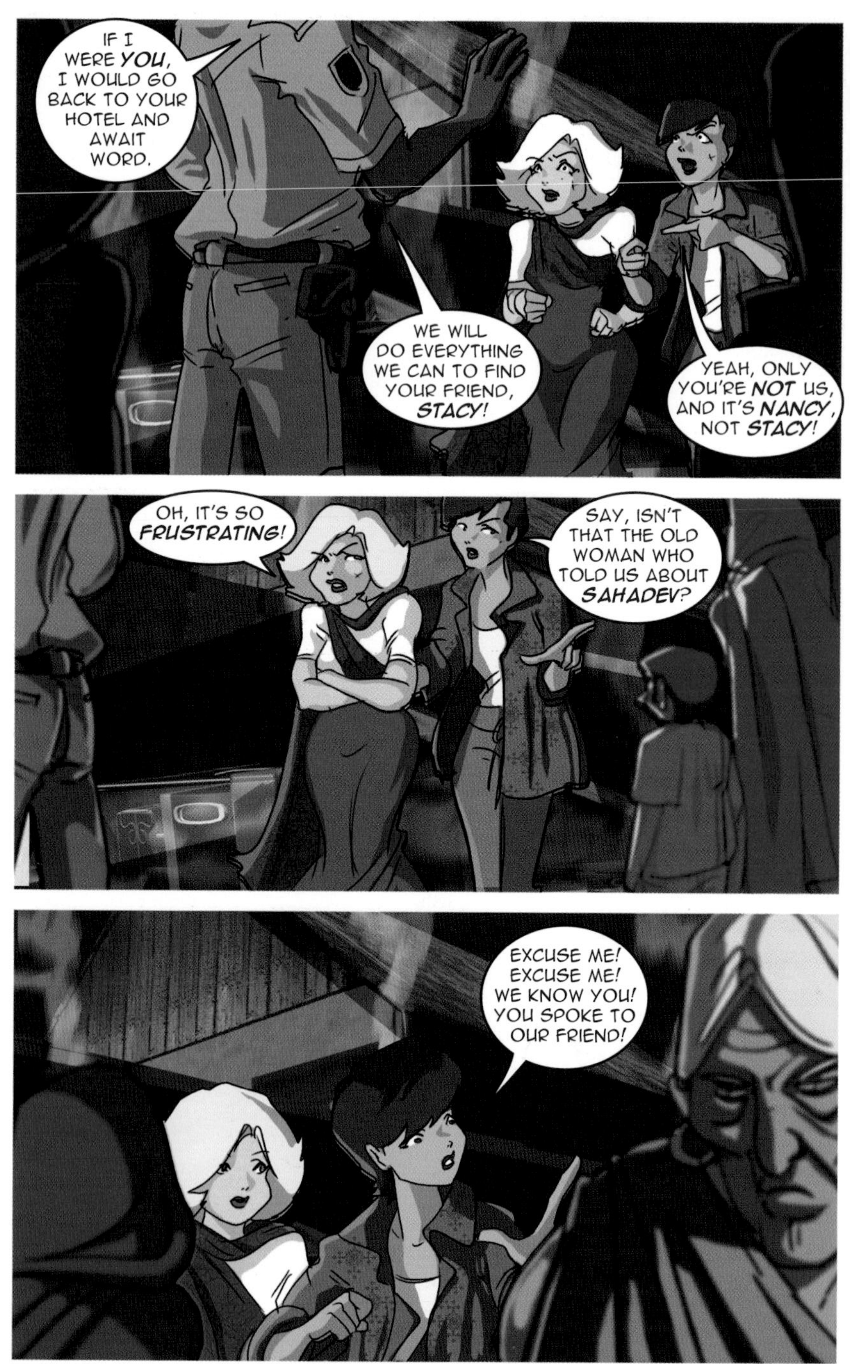
IF I WERE YOU, I WOULD GO BACK TO YOUR HOTEL AND AWAIT WORD.
WE WILL DO EVERYTHING WE CAN TO FIND YOUR FRIEND, STACY!
YEAH, ONLY YOU'RE NOT US, AND IT'S NANCY, NOT STACY!
OH, IT'S SO FRUSTRATING!
SAY, ISN'T THAT THE OLD WOMAN WHO TOLD US ABOUT SAHADEV?
EXCUSE ME! EXCUSE ME! WE KNOW YOU! YOU SPOKE TO OUR FRIEND!

YES, AND I WARNED YOU NOT TO GET INVOLVED.
SEE WHAT HAS HAPPENED NOW?
YOU CANNOT TRUST THESE POLICE. THEY BELONG TO SAHADEV!
SO THAT MEANS WE HAVE TO FIND OUR FRIEND.
COULD YOU HELP US? COULD YOU TRANSLATE THIS DIARY FOR US?
ALL RIGHT.

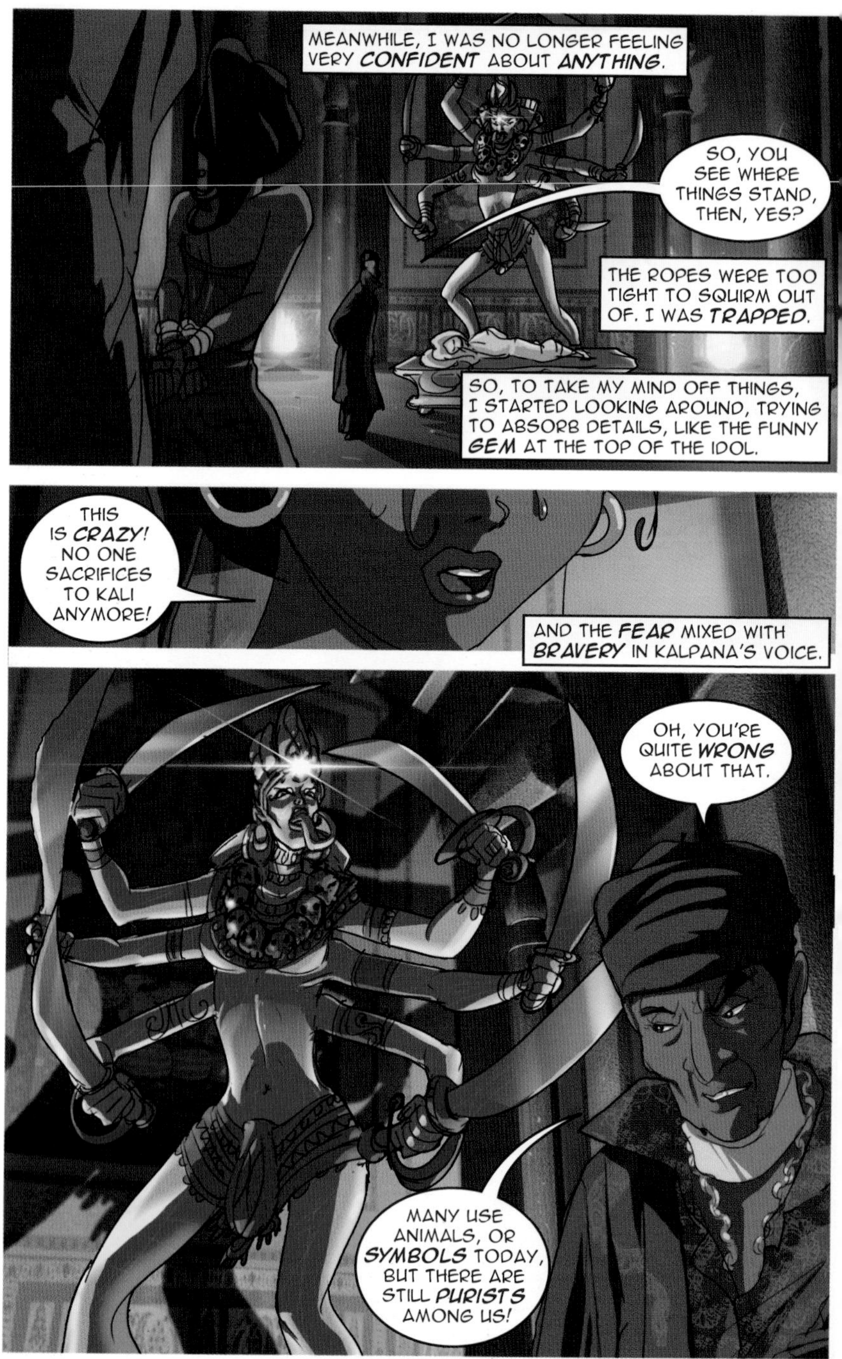
MEANWHILE, I WAS NO LONGER FEELING VERY CONFIDENT ABOUT ANYTHING.
SO, YOU SEE WHERE THINGS STAND, THEN, YES?
THE ROPES WERE TOO TIGHT TO SQUIRM OUT OF. I WAS TRAPPED.
SO, TO TAKE MY MIND OFF THINGS, I STARTED LOOKING AROUND, TRYING TO ABSORB DETAILS, LIKE THE FUNNY GEM AT THE TOP OF THE IDOL.
THIS IS CRAZY! NO ONE SACRIFICES TO KALI ANYMORE!
AND THE FEAR MIXED WITH BRAVERY IN KALPANA'S VOICE.
OH, YOU'RE QUITE WRONG ABOUT THAT.
MANY USE ANIMALS, OR SYMBOLS TODAY, BUT THERE ARE STILL PURISTS AMONG US!

BUT IT DOESN'T *HAVE* TO BE THIS WAY!
TELL ME WHICH ONE OF MY MEN IS YOUR FATHER, AND I PROMISE I WILL LET ALL *THREE* OF YOU GO!
AND THE WAY EVERYTHING SAHADEV SAID SOUNDED LIKE A *LIE*. I WASN'T SURE HE'D *REALLY* KILL ME, BUT I HAD A HUNCH KALPANA'S *FATHER* WOULDN'T LIVE IF HE FOUND HIM.
NO! I WILL *NEVER* BETRAY MY FATHER!
THEN IT IS DECIDED...

OF COURSE, YOU CAN ONLY KEEP YOURSELF DISTRACTED FOR SO LONG...
NANCY DREW MUST DIE!
END CHAPTER TWO

TAKE THAT YOU OLD AUTO-RICKSHAW ENGINE!
WHAK
CHUGGA
CHUGGA
CHUGGA
WHADDAYA KNOW? IT WORKED! NOW AT LEAST WE CAN GIVE THIS BACK TO THE OWNER, IF WE CAN FIND HIM!
HOW'S THE TRANSLATION COMING, GEORGE?
I KEEP SAYING I CAN ONLY TYPE SO FAST, BUT SHE WON'T LISTEN!
"DARSHAN WORKS FOR SAHADEV! I SAW THEM TALK! TO THINK, I ALMOST LET HIM KISS ME! NO WONDER HE KEPT ASKING ABOUT MY FATHER!"

CHAPTER THREE:
A NOT-SO REAL GEM
"HE WANTS TO MEET ME TONIGHT BY THE PARK IN THE CORPORATE CENTER, BUT I'M AFRAID."
"I WISH THERE WERE TIME TO ASK NANCY DREW WHAT TO DO. SHE SEEMS TOO SMART TO GET HERSELF INTO THIS KIND OF DANGEROUS SITUATION!"
HMM... DOESN'T KNOW OUR NANCY SO WELL, DOES SHE?
HEADLIGHTS! MAYBE IT'S MR. DREW! IT FEELS LIKE HOURS SINCE WE CALLED!
HEADS UP, BESS. HE SAID HE'D BRING THE POLICE, BUT THAT DOESN'T LOOK LIKE A POLICE CAR!
UH-OH.
SAY, ISN'T THAT THE SAME VAN THAT TOOK NANCY?

YES! IT IS!
DUCK!

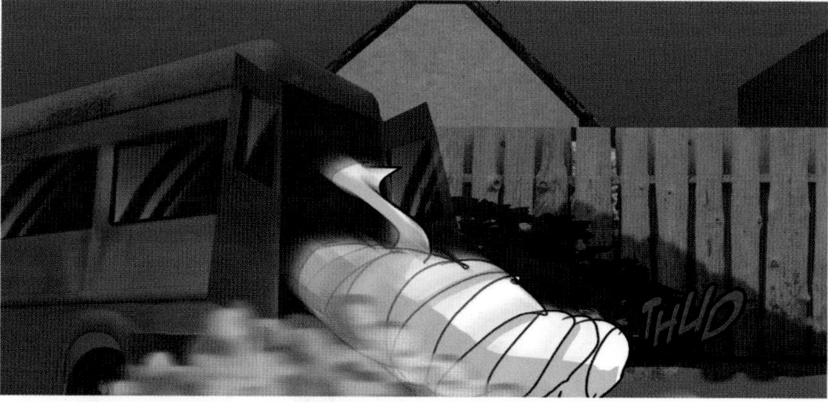
THUD

GEORGE! IS THAT... IS THAT...?
NANCY? YIKES!
I WARNED YOU! I WARNED YOU! NOW YOUR FRIEND IS DEAD! AIEEEE!

MMMF
NOT QUITE DEAD! BESS, HURRY UP AND GIVE ME A HAND WITH THESE SHEETS!
BESS! GEORGE! ARE YOU GUYS A SIGHT FOR SORE EYES!
AND I DO MEAN SORE! I FEEL PRETTY BRUISED!
ARE YOU OKAY? WE WERE WORRIED SICK!
WELL, I WAS KIDNAPPED, TOSSED IN A DUNGEON AND ALMOST SACRIFICED TO THE GODDESS KALI! AND THAT'S NOT THE WORST PART.
KALPANA IS STILL BEING HELD!

YOU FOUND HER?
MORE LIKE I WAS TAKEN BY THE SAME PEOPLE WHO TOOK HER.
SAHADEV WANTS TO FORCE HER TO CONFESS WHICH ONE OF HIS MEN IS SECRETLY HER DAD.
HIS HENCHMAN VARIYA ACTED LIKE HE WAS GOING TO KILL ME UP UNTIL THE LAST MINUTE...
BUT I GUESS EVEN HE DIDN'T WANT A MURDER ON HIS HEAD!
WHOK
BUT NOW THAT YOU KNOW WHERE SHE IS, WE CAN TELL THE POLICE! THEY'RE ALREADY ON THE WAY WITH YOUR DAD!
I WISH! I WAS BLINDFOLDED FOR THE FIRST TRIP AND WRAPPED IN A SHEET FOR THE SECOND.
POOR KALPANA, I HAVE NO IDEA WHERE SHE IS!

MAYBE THIS WILL HELP. WE HAD HER DIARY TRANSLATED INTO ENGLISH.
A CLUE! OH, YOU GUYS ARE THE BEST!
WE KNOW!
AHA!
THE NIGHT OF HER DISAPPEARANCE, KALPANA WAS SUPPOSED TO MEET DARSHAN IN A PARK!
I'VE GOT A HUNCH THAT'S WHERE THEY WANTED TO KIDNAP HER, BUT WHEN SHE DIDN'T SHOW UP, THEY HAD TO CHANGE THEIR PLANS AND TAKE HER FROM HER HOME!
I'M BETTING THAT PARK IS NEAR THEIR CROOKED HQ!
WE'VE GOT TO GET BACK TO GURGUAN, FAST!

SAY, WHERE'S THE DRIVER?
LET'S JUST SAY THERE'S GOING TO BE A BIG TAXI BILL WHEN THIS IS DONE.
AND WE CAN'T JUST LEAVE! LIKE I SAID, YOUR DAD'S ON THE WAY HERE WITH THE POLICE!
SO LET'S CALL HIM!
UM... CELLS DON'T WORK, REMEMBER? IT WAS HARD ENOUGH GETTING SOMEONE TO LOAN US A PHONE THE FIRST TIME! THEY'RE ALL AFRAID OF SAHADEV!
WHO KNOWS WHAT THEY'LL DO TO POOR KALPANA! I'LL GO AHEAD - YOU TWO STAY AND BRING THE CAVALRY!
BUT WE'RE A TEAM!
ALWAYS! BUT SNEAKING IS EASIER FOR ONE!
LOAN ME SOME NAIL POLISH, BESS!
ODD TIME TO THINK OF YOUR LOOKS, BUT I APPROVE!
NO! I WANT SOMETHING TO LEAVE YOU GUYS AS A CLUE WHEN I FIND THE CROOK'S HIDEOUT!

I DROVE THE AUTO-RICKSHAW AS CLOSE TO THE PARK AS I DARED, THEN WALKED THE LAST MILE.
THE PLACE WAS PRETTY CREEPY AT NIGHT. EVEN THE MONKEYS SEEMED ON EDGE.
ASIDE FROM MYSELF AND MY SIMIAN PALS, THE PARK WAS EMPTY, EXCEPT FOR A FEW MEN STANDING BY A PORTABLE OUTHOUSE.
BUT THEN...
I WONDERED, HOW COULD FOUR MEN SQUEEZE INTO THAT LITTLE BATHROOM? UNLESS...
I'D FOUND THE HIDEOUT!

THE QUESTION WAS, HOW WAS *I* GOING TO GET IN WITHOUT BEING SEEN?

I MUST'VE SEEN *THIS* TRICK LIKE A *MILLION* TIMES.

WHAT WAS THAT?
PROBABLY SOME OF THOSE LOUSY *MONKEYS*.

YOU'D THINK BY NOW THAT NO SELF-RESPECTING CROOK WOULD *EVER* FALL FOR IT AGAIN.

BUT SOMETIMES, THE *OLDIES* ARE THE *GOODIES!* AND, AFTER ALL, MANY CRIMINALS DON'T HAVE THE MOST *THOROUGH* EDUCATION.

SAHADEV HAS A *BIG DELIVERY* PLANNED TONIGHT. WE CAN'T AFFORD ANY MISTAKES. BETTER CHECK IT OUT.

A BIG DELIVERY? SOMETHING CROOKED, I BET. I'D HEARD THAT SAHADEV WAS A SMUGGLER.
MAYBE THIS WAS WHAT KALPANA'S DAD WAS WAITING FOR BEFORE REVEALING HIMSELF AND ARRESTING SAHADEV!
I DIDN'T HAVE MUCH TIME TO THINK ABOUT IT RIGHT THEN AND THERE. THOSE THUGS WOULD BE BACK ANY SECOND.
AND FIRST I HAD TO LEAVE A CLUE!
BESS AND GEORGE WOULD KNOW THAT ND WAS ME, AND NN WAS MY BOYFRIEND, NED NICKERSON!
I ONLY HOPED THEY'D ALSO REALIZE CUPID'S ARROW WAS POINTED RIGHT AT THE DOOR TO THE HIDEOUT!

PAY DIRT! I'D STUMBLED ONTO A MAJOR OPERATION! SAHADEV WAS DEALING IN PIRATED DVDS!

TO APPRECIATE HOW ***BIG*** THIS WAS, YOU'D HAVE TO KNOW INDIA'S FILM INDUSTRY (NAMED ***BOLLYWOOD***, AFTER... WELL, HOLLYWOOD) IS ONE OF THE LARGEST IN THE WORLD.

IF AN UNSCRUPULOUS CROOK CAN STEAL AN UNRELEASED MOVIE, THEY CAN CREATE THEIR OWN BOOTLEG DVDS AND MAKE MILLIONS SELLING THEM ILLEGALLY.

BOOTLEGGING CAN COST LEGITIMATE FILMMAKERS ***MILLIONS*** IN LOST SALES!

I WAS SO BUSY PIECING THIS MYSTERY TOGETHER, I BARELY NOTICED I WAS TRAPPED!
I COULDN'T GO DOWN, BECAUSE EVERYONE WOULD SEE ME! I COULDN'T GO UP, BECAUSE THE GUARDS HAD RETURNED! AND I COULDN'T STAY, BECAUSE THE MEN WERE STARTING TO CARRY THE CRATES OUT.
BUT... IF YOU CAN'T GO UP OR DOWN, SOMETIMES YOU HAVE TO GO THROUGH! THINKING FAST,I SLIPPED BETWEEN THE STEPS, BARELY IN TIME.
MY FINGERS WEREN'T STRONG ENOUGH TO LET ME HANG AROUND FOREVER, SO I MADE A QUICK JUMP TO THE FLOOR.

THE BEST WAY TO FALL IS TO TRY TO ROLL WHEN YOU HIT THE GROUND, TO ABSORB SOME OF THE MOMENTUM.
I WISH I'D REMEMBERED THAT, BECAUSE I HIT THE GROUND LIKE A REAL AMATEUR!
THIS WAS NO TIME TO FEEL SORRY FOR MYSELF THOUGH. THERE WAS KALPANA!
NANCY!
SHHH!
EVERYONE'S BUSY, BUT THEY WON'T BE FOREVER, SO WE'VE GOT JUST A FEW SECONDS TO GET YOU OUT OF HERE!
GREAT! BUT HOW? WE'RE TOTALLY SURROUND-ED!

HMM... THEY'RE CARRYING THOSE **CRATES** OUT. WHY DON'T WE JUST GET **IN** ONE?
DO YOU THINK WE'LL BOTH FIT?
WE'LL HAVE TO! HURRY!

MMMF!

IT LOOKED BIGGER FROM OUTSIDE. SORRY IF MY FOOT IS IN YOUR SIDE.
JUST DON'T MOVE IT. I'M TICKLISH. HEE-HEE!
SHH! FOOT-STEPS!
THIS ONE NEXT?
WHY NOT?
UNGH! THIS ONE'S HEAVIER THAN THE OTHERS!
STOP COMPLAINING AND WORK!

CAREFUL! HOLD ON!
I WAS THINKING MAYBE IF OUR LIVES WEREN'T IN DANGER...
IT'S SLIPPING, I TELL YOU!
OKAY, OKAY! LET'S FLIP IT TO GET A BETTER GRIP.
...THIS WHOLE THING MIGHT SEEM FUNNY...
THAT'S BETTER!
SORT OF.

OF COURSE, WHEN SAHADEV HIMSELF PULLED THE CRATE OPEN, IT WASN'T FUNNY AT ALL.
GET OUT. NOW.
DID YOU REALLY THINK YOU COULD ESCAPE ME?
I SOMETIMES WONDER WHY CROOKS ASK SUCH SILLY QUESTIONS. OF COURSE WE THOUGHT WE COULD ESCAPE. WHY ELSE WOULD WE TRY?
I KNOW MS. NANCY DREW HAS A REPUTATION BACK HOME, BUT THIS IS NOT HER HOME!
MY SHIPMENT IS ON ITS WAY. KALPANA'S FATHER AND ALL THE POLICE IN THE WORLD CAN NO LONGER STOP IT, SO, THERE'S NO REASON TO KEEP YOU TWO ALIVE ANYMORE!

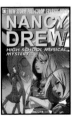

Available on the iPad
App Store

Nancy Drew: Ghost of Thornton Hall

Some Families Keep Deadly Secrets!

Jessalyn Thornton's fateful sleepover at the abandoned Thornton estate was supposed to be a pre-wedding celebration, but the fun ended when she disappeared. While her family searches for clues, others refuse to speak about the estate's dark past. Did something supernatural happen to Jessalyn, or is someone in Thornton Hall holding something besides family secrets?